One Dead Dean

Also by Bill Crider

Too Late to Die
Shotgun Saturday Night
Cursed to Death

One Dead Dean

Bill Crider

Walker and Company
New York

First published in the United States of America in 1988 by the Walker Publishing Company, Inc.

Published simultaneously in Canada by Thomas Allen & Son Canada, Limited, Markham, Ontario.

Library of Congress Cataloging-in-Publication Data
Crider, Bill, 1941
One dead dean.

I. Title.
PS3553.R497O54 1988   813'.54   88-134
ISBN 0-8027-5711-1

Printed in the United States of America
10 9 8 7 6 5 4 3 2 1

This Book Is For: Billy and Charlotte
Peter and Evelyn
Joe and Al
Pat and Beverly
Gene and Suzi
Charlie and Jeanne
Groner and J.B.
Tessica

Prologue

ONE HOT AUGUST night in 1897 Hartley Gorman got saved in the Pearly Gates Baptist Church. Within thirty minutes of the time he walked the aisle for Jesus, the preacher had him totally immersed in the murky waters of Orchard Creek. On the banks, watching avidly an event that most of them thought they'd never live to see, was most of the population of Pecan City, Texas, having piled into wagons, buckboards, surreys, gigs, and one-horse shays to get there in time.

When Hartley Gorman walked out on the bank, mud sucking at his church-going shoes, water dripping from his sodden pants legs and running in streams out of his hair and down his face, he was vouchsafed a vision. He fell to his knees, threw up his arms, and pitched face forward on the creek bank. He was speaking aloud, but no one could understand the words, Gorman's mouth being mostly full of muddy grass at the time. Nobody dared to turn him over while he was in the grip of the Holy Spirit.

He told everybody who would listen later that he'd seen the Lord (though he was always a little vague on what He looked like), who had commanded him to build a school, a college where ladies and gentlemen could go to learn without being tainted by the evil influences of the World, the Flesh, and the Devil, three things that most people in Pecan City thought Hartley Gorman knew plenty about himself. Not that he ever had anything to do with them again.

In fact, Hartley Gorman became a saintly man, dedicated to his dream, which, thanks to the fact that Hartley was by far the richest man in Pecan City, soon had become a reality.

1

By late the following fall, a little over a year after his vision, Hartley Gorman College's first building was standing in all its glory, three stories high, with a veneer of native sandstone and a tall steeple on top. Twenty-two students had enrolled.

Twenty years later, when Gorman died, the school, not having grown very much, was taken over by his denomination. Eventually, new buildings were added and more students came, but the school remained small and isolated, known mostly for its occasional powerhouse basketball teams. Nothing very remarkable ever happened there, no Rhodes scholars got sent to Britain, no astronauts were graduated. Hartley Gorman College remained a quiet, undistinguished school, safe from its founder's three bugaboos, or relatively safe at least—a place that few, if any, outside the state had ever heard of. It stayed that way for a long, long time.

1

DURING THE TEN-minute break between his nine and ten o'clock classes, Carl Burns sat in his office working on his list of things he hated. He had just written down *Dental floss that shreds between your back teeth* and was starting on *People who fart in elevators* when his student secretary walked into his office.

His secretary's name—her honest-to-God name, right there on all her official records and, Burns supposed, on her birth certificate as well—was Bunni. With an *i*. Burns shuddered to think what her parents must be like. He hoped he'd never have to meet them.

Aside from her name, however, Bunni had certain assets, assets of the kind to make male professors—even male professors at Hartley Gorman College—snap their heads around in the hallways. There was her flawless, creamy skin. Her long blonde hair. Her blue, blue eyes. Her pneumatic breasts. Only two things restrained Burns from leaping across his massive brown executive desk and attempting to rip off her skintight Gloria Vanderbilts with his teeth: (1) He would certainly be fired for moral turpitude, and (2) she chewed gum. *People who chew gum in public* were high on the list Burns was working on.

"Hi, Dr. Burns," Bunni said, giving her gum a good workout. Juicy Fruit. Burns particularly hated the odor of Juicy Fruit gum. "Dean Elmore called while you were in class."

Burns looked up at her and then down his list. He drew a line through the word *People*, which was as far as he'd gotten with the sentence he'd begun earlier, and wrote *Dean Elmore* in his neat, precise hand. Then he drew a long, looping arrow from Elmore's name to near the top of the list, the arrowhead pointing to the space between *People who talk aloud in movie theaters* and *Days when the humidity is more than 40%*.

He put the cap on his black-ink-filled Pilot Precise Ball Liner and looked back up at Bunni. "And what did the Dear Departed say that he wanted to see me about?"

A cloud crossed the clear blue sky of Bunni's eyes. Burns knew that he was wrong to joke about Elmore's appearance with her, since Bunni seldom understood a joke. Besides, Elmore almost certainly hadn't said what he wanted, one of his favorite tactics being to instill doubt in anyone he could, at any time, about anything at all.

But this time Burns was surprised. Not only had Elmore left a message, Bunni had remembered it. "It was just a reminder call," she said. "About the luncheon today."

"Ah," Burns said. "The luncheon. Thank you, Bunni, for bringing that message. You run along to class now. I'll be in soon." Bunni was in his ten o'clock American literature class. "Today I'm going to give you a list of ten characteristics of Romanticism. You get ready to write them down."

Bunni's eyes cleared. "Yes, sir," she said, and left the office.

Burns smiled. One of the things he liked about Hartley Gorman College was the fact that the students there still knew how to say "sir" with some degree of sincerity. One of the things he didn't like was the Friday "luncheons," supposedly a time for the academic dean to hear reports from the various department heads, but mostly a time for Elmore to berate, humiliate, and castigate his staff instead. It was not an event that Burns looked forward to with eager anticipation. In fact he felt a lot like a man Mark Twain had described, a man who was about to be hanged, who said that if it weren't for the honor of the thing, he'd just as soon skip it.

4

Burns gathered up the textbook and his notes from the top of his desk. Then he opened the wide, thin drawer in the middle of the desk and tossed in his list of things he hated. He could work on it some more later in the day. He tossed in the black Pilot, too. For his class rolls, he used a Paper Mate Power Point that Bunni had given him for Christmas the year before.

He wondered who would get the reaming at the luncheon later that day. Burns couldn't recall having done anything himself, but at dear old Hartley Gorman College, you didn't actually have to be guilty of doing something to get a reaming. That was another of Elmore's tactics. He liked to keep people off balance.

As Burns stood wondering, the bell rang to signal the beginning of class. He could reach his classroom in seconds, but the route was complicated. His office was on the third floor of the school's original building, now almost ninety years old. Its official designation was "Hartley Gorman I"— all the buildings were, for some reason, numbered—but it was called simply "Main" by almost everyone—except, of course, for Elmore, who prided himself on knowing the numbers of all the buildings and who never referred to them any other way. Burns's office was Main 301, slightly isolated since it was in what appeared to have been designed originally as an elevator shaft.

Burns didn't mind that his office stuck out on the side of the building above one other office and an entryway. What he minded was what was over his head, and the maze he had to run to get to class. Main's third floor, which had served as the college's chapel in its early years, had been remodeled for the Psychology Department some years before and eventually inherited by the English Department when psych moved to newer, plusher quarters.

Burns had to leave his office, go through a narrow hallway past the usually open doors of two small classrooms (used as observation rooms by psych), turn left, walk past two tiny offices, turn left, turn right again almost immediately, cross a wide hall, and enter his classroom. A rat could hardly run the maze any better.

The Psych Department was also responsible for what was over Burns's head when he sat at his desk—namely, hundreds of pounds of pigeon shit. Burns had been assured by Mal Tomlin that the shit was real. "See," Mal had said, puffing madly on his hundred-millimeter cigarette, "the Psych guys had to have pigeons for their experiments. So they left the attic windows open and put out grain up there. Then when they needed a few pigeons, they'd go up and club 'em. I've been up there, kid. I know what I'm talking about. If that ceiling of yours ever collapses while you're in the chair behind your desk, you'll be five feet deep in the stuff. Don't count on *me* to dig you out. I expect they'll just lock your office door and put a little plaque on it, like they did in the song for Big Bad John."

Burns was never sure when Mal was lying, but he was never very comfortable sitting in his office. Well, he couldn't worry about that now. He walked into his class, checked the roll, and began his list. The students were ready for him, and they began taking down everything he said.

After class, Burns stopped in the first office on his way back, the office of Clementine Nelson. She was "Clem" to everyone except Elmore, who had the irritating habit of calling everyone by his or her complete Christian name when he deigned to use the Christian name at all.

Clem was a compact woman of about fifty with short hair that she brushed straight back from her face. She had very clear brown eyes, and she always wore severely tailored skirts and blouses in tones of khaki and brown. She looked to Burns like a retired semipro shortstop.

Clem was at her desk grading papers. Burns leaned in the door frame. "I really punished them today," he said.

Clem looked up. "Another one of your famous lists?"

6

"Right. You should have seen them taking it down. You would have thought it was the holy writ."

Clem laid down her red pen on the stack of papers. "You remember what it was like ten or fifteen years ago? Always questions. Those kids really kept you on your toes."

"I remember," Burns said. "Now the only question anyone has is "How will all this help me get a better job and make over fifty thousand a year?""

"What do you tell them?"

"I used to tell them that anything that made them more human was worth studying for its own sake and that money didn't mean as much as they thought it did. Some of them even believed me."

"But what do you tell them now?"

"Now I don't tell them anything. The smart ones will figure it out for themselves."

"Ha." Burns couldn't interpret the "Ha," so he didn't say anything.

"You have your weekly meeting today?" Clem asked.

"As usual," Burns said. "Neither rain, nor hail, nor dark of night . . ."

". . . shall keep you from your appointed scolding," Clem said. "Give Elmore my love."

"Naturally," Burns said. Clem and Elmore had been involved in a difference of opinion in a committee meeting three years before, shortly after Elmore's appointment as dean. Elmore had addressed the faculty, emphasizing his open-mindedness and his ability to see both sides of a question. "We can agree to disagree," he said. Three days later, Clem had disagreed. Thirty minutes after *that*, Elmore had gone to the president and tried to get her fired. The fact that he had not succeeded had only increased his dislike of her.

Burns pushed away from the door frame, took two steps, stuck his head in the next office, said "Hello, Miss Darling," and kept going. Miss Darling, as far as Burns knew, seldom spoke to anyone. She was long past the regular retirement

7

age, and Burns thought she was quite dotty. He knew of at least one freshman comp class that she had entered and proceeded to teach a lesson on Shakespeare that was supposed to be taught in her sophomore British literature class. The freshmen sat politely through it all. Burns had mentioned Miss Darling to Elmore in his faculty evaluation memo, but Elmore had done nothing. Elmore, in fact, loved Miss Darling, who never spoke up in faculty meetings, never crossed anyone up in committees, and never questioned any administrative decision, no matter how lunatic it may have seemed to the rest of the faculty. Miss Darling could go on teaching the wrong lesson to the wrong class well into the next century and Elmore would never dream of replacing her.

Another two steps and Burns had turned the corner to the hall leading to his own office. Waiting inside was Earl Fox, chairman of the History Department, which was housed on the second floor. "Got any matches?" Earl asked.

"I think so," Burns said, walking past Fox and around his desk. He opened the drawer into which he'd tossed his list and rummaged around until he found a matchbook advertising Hernando's Fine Mexican Food. He handed it to Fox.

"Let's go down for a smoke," Fox said.

Fox and Burns had come to Hartley Gorman College the same year, 1973, a time when English and history teachers were a dime a dozen, a time when there were often hundreds of applicants for every job that opened. They had been hired at HGC simply because many people had never heard of the place, and many others didn't think they could work under the restrictive conditions of a denominational school. Still others thought they were too good to waste away in a tiny college of no prestige located hundreds of miles from anywhere on the eastern edge of West Texas.

The rules, however, were not really as restrictive as people sometimes thought. Smoking, for instance, was permitted on campus; but Fox didn't like to be seen smoking. He and

Burns generally smoked in the history lounge, a small, unused office on the second floor.

As they walked down the stairs, Fox said, "Thank God the football season's over."

"It hasn't been over long enough," Burns said. In fact, the HGC Panthers had lost their last game of the season only the previous Saturday, by a score of forty-eight to nothing. They had also lost the ten previous games, most of them by a similar score. Each passing week had seen Elmore's comments in the weekly luncheon grow more scathing as he addressed the coach, who was also the head of the Physical Education Department.

No one was in the history lounge when they reached it. No one usually was. The room was small and bleak, with the paint peeling off the walls, and it was lit by a single hundred-watt bulb hanging at the end of a fraying brown fabric-covered cord that dangled from the twelve-foot ceiling. The furnishings consisted entirely of items that Fox had picked up at garage sales: an ancient card table with the blue lamination peeling from its cardboard top, three steel chairs even older than the table, and a ghastly floral couch with a missing cushion, covered with unidentifiable stains.

Fox loved garage sales, and he usually looked as if he bought all his clothes at them. Today he was wearing a pair of double-knit pants decorated with huge windowpane checks of brown, green, red, and gray, a knit shirt with a penguin on the pocket, and a Dallas Cowboys windbreaker. One of the windbreaker pockets had been partially ripped away, there were ink stains on the shirt, and the fly of the pants would zip only about three-quarters of the way to the top. All of this was in distinct contrast with Fox's head and face. His clean-cut features and razor-cut hair would not have looked out of place in a preppie handbook.

Fox closed the door of the lounge as Burns sat down in one of the steel chairs. Then Fox sat in one of the other chairs and pulled out a crumpled pack of L & Ms from the unripped pocket of the windbreaker. He offered the pack to Burns, who took one, more to be companionable than because he wanted to smoke. Burns never smoked except when he was with Fox or Mal Tomlin.

They lit up with Burns's matches and smoked in silence for a minute, tapping their ashes into a red and white Diet Coke can that sat in the middle of the card table. They knew that there was little likelihood that they would be disturbed. Dean Elmore had long ago made known in an open faculty meeting his opinions about "the malcontent mutterings of lugubrious lounge lizards," and shortly thereafter the lounge once used by the general faculty had been converted into a meeting place for the student government.

"You know, you're right," Fox said, taking a deep drag on his L & M. "Elmore will probably let Coach Thomas have it again today. I hate to say it, but I guess that's better than one of us getting a going-over."

Burns tapped ashes into the Coke can. He knew what Fox meant. Elmore had several times made scathing remarks about Fox's wardrobe and attacked the History Department in general for its "low standards of personal conduct," which Burns interpreted to mean that Elmore knew that Fox smoked in the history lounge. "E pluribus unum," Burns said.

"Don't give me that crap," Fox said, dropping his cigarette butt into the can and reaching into his pocket for the pack. "You know as well as I do that there's no unity around here. Everyone is just looking for some way to stick it to somebody else. Nobody's interested in anything except saving his own job." He lit the cigarette that he had shaken out of the pack. "Present company excepted, of course." He blew out a long plume of smoke.

"Of course," Burns said, dropping his own butt into the can. He was well aware that HGC was working under strict budget limitations. In the past few years, there had been a considerable drop in enrollment, mostly due to Elmore, in

10

Burns's opinion, and there was a concerted effort under way to reduce the size of the faculty. And Elmore had a pretty good idea of whom he wanted to send away.

Fox pushed back his chair and propped his feet up on the table, a precarious proposition. He seemed quite comfortable, however. Burns noted that he was wearing a pair of Hush Puppies that had probably never been brushed. They were the dirtiest Hush Puppies that Burns had ever seen. The sole of the left shoe had separated from the upper at the toe. "Heard the latest?" Fox asked after achieving a satisfactory balance.

"Probably not," Burns said. He was pretty sure that he was always the last to hear any of the campus gossip. Once when a math teacher had been fired, the man had been gone for three months before Burns even heard about the incident.

"L. J.'s got a job at North Texas State," Fox said.

L. J. was L. J. Hitt, a psychology teacher whom Burns knew slightly. "How'd he luck into that?" Burns asked.

"Don't know," Fox said. "All I know is that he's leaving at midterm."

"How many does that make now?"

"Right at forty," Fox said.

"Hard to believe," Burns said, shaking his head. "Give me another cigarette."

Fox handed him the pack and Burns lit up, thinking about the forty or so faculty members who had been fired, quit, resigned, or retired since Elmore's ascendancy to the deanship.

"Why don't we leave?" Fox asked. It wasn't a rhetorical question.

"Four reasons," Burns said through a haze of cigarette smoke. "One: We're having too much fun. Two: We can't believe Elmore would really fire *us*. Three: In our fields, it's almost impossible to find jobs. And four: We don't have the guts."

"You and your damned lists," Fox said. "I guess that about

11

covers it, though. Still, it wouldn't hurt to look around."

"I look in the job vacancies section of the *Chronicle of Higher Education* every two weeks," Burns said. "Don't you?"

"Yeah," Fox said. "For all the good it does."

"I'll tell you how mine read," Burns said. " 'Position for specialist in American literature. Nontenure track. Prestigious publications required. Ph.D. required. Load will consist of five courses in freshman composition. Some off-campus teaching'—that means you get to teach in the local units of the Texas penal system—'required. Salary, seventeen five to eighteen five per year, depending on experience.' "

"I think you're probably exaggerating," Fox said. "But not by much."

"Not much at all," Burns said, dropping his second butt in the Coke can. "Let's go to the luncheon."

2

ON THEIR WAY out of Main, they were joined by Mal Tomlin. Mal was the chairman of the Education Department, which occupied the first floor. He was smoking a Merit Menthol 100. Mal smoked anywhere he pleased, and he didn't care who knew it. He was a compact, muscular man, who looked even more like a former semipro shortstop than Clementine Nelson did. "You fellas want a cigarette?" he asked. He took out his Merit pack and offered it to Fox, who waved it away. Tomlin took great pleasure in offering Fox cigarettes in public, knowing that Fox would never take one. "Wonder who'll go on the firing line today?" he said, replacing his cigarettes in his shirt pocket.

"Could be any of us," Burns said. "As usual."

Mal shook his head ruefully. He knew as well as anyone how Elmore could cut someone down. He had been the target only two weeks before, when Elmore had lashed out at the Education Department as being the refuge of fifth-rate students with tenth-rate minds and ambitions that rated so low they couldn't be measured. "The dregs!" Elmore had yelled. "The very dregs! That's who signs up for education courses! And they pass! Can any of you believe that? They all pass!"

Mal had tried to explain that any student entering the teacher-education program had to be carrying a 2.0 average in all his other courses, but it had done no good. Elmore's plan to improve the education curriculum was simple: Add another year. Make the prospective teachers spend five years in school instead of four. When Mal had said that teachers were already grossly underpaid and that hardly anyone would want to attend school for an extra year in anticipation of earning a teacher's salary, Elmore had exploded again. "Idiots! If they could get any other job, they wouldn't want to teach in the first place."

Elmore was a warm and understanding man.

As they passed the Bible Building (Hartley Gorman IX, in Elmore's terminology), Abner Swan came down the walk and fell in with them. The chairman of the Bible Department, Swan was widely regarded as the biggest ass-kisser in the known universe. Whenever Elmore was to be agreed with, Swan could be counted on for a resounding "Amen!" If anyone dared to question Elmore (a rare occurrence, but it happened) Swan could be counted on to glare at the questioner as if glaring at the pope. Or the Devil.

"A beautiful day, eh, gentlemen?" Swan boomed.

As a matter of fact, it was not a beautiful day. The sky was thickly overcast, the temperature was around forty degrees, and there was a brisk north wind that cut right through everyone's clothes, particularly Fox's double-knit pants. But that didn't bother Swan. He was out to curry favor with all and sundry, even God.

"Yeah, Abner, it's lovely," Burns said.

"Yes, indeed," Swan said, "a day to be truly thankful for." He rubbed his hands together like Uriah Heep, though Burns had never considered Swan a model of humility, even of false humility. What Burns liked about Swan was his clothes. Today he was wearing a navy blue knit suit, a pale yellow shirt, a flowing navy and yellow tie, and white patent leather shoes. His hair was cut by a barber who had carefully studied the finest in television evangelist hairstyles.

Swan cut a fine figure. He was big—three or four inches over six feet—and he loved getting his picture in the local papers. When the Bible Building (or Hartley Gorman IX) had been constructed a few years previously, Swan had, in the words of Mal Tomlin, "worn overalls every day and lurked around the construction site waiting for a photographer to show up."

Not that any of this saved Swan from Elmore's wrath. When Swan had worn his overalls to a Friday luncheon, Elmore had called him a "bumptious boob." He had ragged him unmercifully when one of the Bible majors, a senior who would have been graduating with honors in a few months, had gotten two girls pregnant, one of them the daughter of a local minister. Through it all, Swan had sat with clenched teeth, his face a deep, dark shade of red. And by the next meeting, his smile would be back in place and his "Amen" would boom out.

They reached the dining hall, which was itself on the first floor of the Men's Dormitory (Hartley Gorman V), and went in by the side door. To the right was the faculty dining room, which the faculty was allowed to use only if attending official meetings called by the dean or the president.

Burns led the way to the back of the room, where a buffet table had been set up, and began filling a plate with rubbery English peas, watery mashed potatoes, wilted salad, and ham that had a slightly greenish tinge around the edges.

Other department heads were already sitting at the dining table. Dick Hayes, from business; Faye Smith, from math and science; Joe Reasoner, from psych; and Coach Thomas. Just coming in the door were Don Elliott, speech and drama; Fran Stafford, languages; and Mary Winsor, journalism. That would be all except for the dean and president, who always came a bit late.

Everyone was aware that this lateness was a deliberate power ploy on the part of Elmore, and that President Rogers was merely playing along. Both men, Rogers especially, were legends of punctuality on the campus, and Rogers was notorious for having students counted absent if they were so much as two minutes late to assembly. Burns thought that Elmore had probably read a book somewhere and gotten the idea that the Big Boss Man never had to be on time to a meet-

15

ing of the Underlings. Why Rogers went along with him was just another mystery.

Sure enough, after everyone was seated and eating, Elmore and President Rogers walked in. The cadaverous Elmore resembled no one so much as John Carradine, as Carradine might have looked with a wavy pompadour liberally coated with daily applications of Grecian Formula. Lay him out in a casket, Burns thought, and he'd make an ideal corpse. His sallow complexion only added to the impression.

President Rogers, on the other hand, was short, dumpy, ruddy, and cheerful, the perfect foil for Elmore in more ways than one. His pleasures seemed to run chiefly to eating, attending the school's sporting events, praying at chapel, and letting Elmore have his way. He was always smiling, had a kind word for everyone, and appeared to be the most harmless of men. Though he was also entirely ineffectual, Hartley Gorman College had muddled along fairly successfully under his presidency for six years, until the advent of Elmore, who had stepped into the power vacuum with a vengeance and proceeded to run the school into the ground.

Why Rogers had let it happen was a question much discussed among the faculty members. No one had an answer. One story had it that Rogers had an incurable disease. Some said that he was senile, though he was only sixty-one. Still others said that a beautiful sophomore had left campus under mysterious circumstances and that Elmore had the goods on someone. Just whom he had the goods on and what the goods were was uncertain.

None of it mattered, in the long run. Elmore had the power. Technically, all decisions had to be approved by the president. In practice, whatever Elmore said, went. As Burns put it to Fox, " 'That is all ye know on earth, and all ye need to know.' "

There was a noticeable lack of small talk at the table. Even the usually irrepressible Mal Tomlin had little to say. Mostly

16

there was the clinking of silverware and the rattle of ice in glasses. The room was always too warm, and condensation formed on the inside of the windows. Finally, Elmore stood. "I'm going to ask Dr. Swan to return thanks," he said.

Swan rose, grateful to be called upon. If he had possessed a tail, he would have wagged it. He launched into a lengthy blessing that included everyone from the president of the United States on down, mentioned the afflicted and the needy, brought in the prosperity of HGC, and concluded by asking a special blessing on Dr. Rogers and Dr. Elmore, "as they guide and direct this great institution dedicated to Thy glory." Burns felt the green ham turning over in his stomach.

"Amen!" boomed Swan. A number of other "Amens" chimed in.

Then Elmore passed around the toothpick holder, a ritual that Burns never failed to view with amazement. Not everyone indulged, of course, but the sight of six or seven adults digging around in their molars with toothpicks was something that required seeing for believing.

After the toothpick ritual was completed, it was time for the dreaded "Departmental Reports," in which each person told what had been accomplished in his area that week. This was when Elmore got rolling. It started with Coach Thomas, who made the rookie mistake of referring to his team's forty-eight to nothing pasting as a "moral victory."

"Moral victory!" Elmore scoffed. "That bunch of refugees from justice wouldn't recognize a moral if it bit them in the gluteus maximus. If they could hang onto a football like they hang onto their girlfriends' mammaries when they strut around campus, we'd be ranked number one in the nation! I would estimate that our alumni contributions to our football program have fallen off by fifty percent in the last two years! Moral victory! One more season of moral victories like that, and ... well, never mind. I don't think we'll have to worry about that."

Coach Thomas sat red-faced and shamed, looking at the

remains of the rubbery peas on his plate, as Elmore went on down the line. Fox got blasted for his Dallas Cowboys windbreaker. "If you can't support your own school, Fox, why take its money?" Tomlin got it for his cigarette. "Only a sick and demented beast fouls its own habitat, Tomlin." Dick Hayes got it for the incompetence (alleged) of a student secretary trained in his department. "She can't even spell her own name the same way twice, much less type a decent business letter. It's quite possible she types with only two fingers; otherwise she could hardly be so slow." Even the local businessmen got it for their tightfistedness. "This town would die without Hartley Gorman College, but these sourballs won't give to support our little scholarship drive. We'll teach them, though. I'm going to pass out a list of everyone who turned us down. I would hope that no one from this school would patronize their businesses."

It went on, but not for as long as usual. Elmore had something else on his mind. "As some of you may know," he said, "our school is in dire financial straits." He stood with arms akimbo and looked hard at each department head. Burns met his eyes. He knew the reason why the school was in trouble.

So did Elmore. "Some of our 'loyal' faculty members have sown the seeds of discord among the students. They have said that the new courses I have introduced into the curriculum—with the complete approval of the Curriculum Committee—will water down their degrees. Make them worthless. I want these faculty members rooted out! They do not belong here at Hartley Gorman!"

Burns was staring straight at Elmore, but he had a powerful desire to stare down at his plate, which is what many of the others were doing. "Complete approval of the Curriculum Committee"—now there was a laugh for you. The committee had fought Elmore from first to last, Clem Nelson almost losing her job in the process, before Elmore had rammed his curriculum through by "Executive Decision."

18

His decision. The committee hadn't even been allowed to vote on the final measure, much less argue against it in a faculty meeting.

The new courses that Elmore was so proud of consisted of such stringent offerings as "Personal Money Management," in which students were required to learn how to balance a checkbook and absorb such gems of wisdom as the fact that clipping newspaper coupons could save them money at the grocery store, especially if the store paid double for each coupon. Then there was the notorious humanities offering, especially hated by Burns, in which students were supposed to get a complete background in twenty centuries or so of music, art, and literature in one semester. Well, Burns thought, it beat learning to balance a checkbook.

Elmore was ranting on. "I have a plan," he said. "A plan to save this school! There are several steps that we can take, beginning with the elimination of major sports, on which we lost over two hundred thousand dollars last year!" So *that* was why there'd be no moral victories.

All eyes, some furtively, some openly, turned to Coach Thomas, who had tried to take a drink of tea, some of which must have gone down the wrong tube. Thomas choked and coughed, slamming his glass down on the table. All the eyes turned away in embarrassment.

Burns sneaked a look at President Rogers. Rogers sat calmly, looking as if his thoughts were on heavenly things, or things at least unrelated to what was happening in the faculty dining room.

"Of course," Elmore said, "such a move must be approved by the board, but I am confident that after I give them my facts and figures they will see things my way. All scholarships will be honored, naturally, but we would seek to hold no athlete here if he or she wished to transfer to another college or university."

Of course, Burns thought. Naturally. But if all the athletes went elsewhere, a considerable portion of the student body

19

would disappear without a trace. What then?

"What then, you ask?" Elmore said, startling Burns badly and causing him to wonder if he had spoken aloud.

"What then?" Elmore repeated. "Let me say now that I have a secret plan, a plan that is both bold and innovative, a plan that will bring thousands and thousands of dollars to this institution each and every semester. It will call for vision, but I believe that we have that vision, and I will be discussing it with you individually in the days to come." He sat down abruptly, leaving everyone to finish his meal, sneak glances at Thomas, and wonder about the "secret plan."

All Burns could think was that the plan, as described by Elmore, must be complete lunacy. There was absolutely no way to bring that much money in without selling off the school's properties, which Burns happened to know had already been done, or by forcing the entire town to enroll for courses.

As soon as possible without seeming too eager, people began to get up and leave the luncheon. As they passed by Elmore, he handed each one a list of businesses that he would prefer they avoid.

3

BURNS HUNG BACK, waiting for Mal Tomlin, who was defiantly finishing another cigarette, and that was how he came to see the confrontation. Most of the other department heads had departed, slinking away as silently and unobtrusively as possible, each one meekly taking the paper that Elmore handed him.

Coach Thomas, however, did not go quietly. He was a big man, who had once had a tryout as an offensive center with the Houston Oilers in the early years of their franchise. He had been one of the last players cut. He had the size, but not the quickness. He had shrunk a little since then, especially in the years since Elmore had been dean, but he was still big. He was wearing a faded HGC letter jacket in the school's colors of black and gold, and his shoulders made any padding superfluous.

Thomas walked up to Elmore, who handed him a piece of paper. Thomas ignored it. "The board will never approve dropping the sports program," he said.

Elmore looked up at him. "Of course they will. It's a losing proposition, and I'll prove it to them. It may be that the football team loses because it's coached by losers, but that doesn't really matter. No one wants to support losers."

Thomas's face was gradually turning a deep, dark red, the red of raw meat laid out in a butcher's shop. As Burns watched, Thomas's fists seemed to grow into hardwood knots, solid as croquet balls and twice as large.

Even President Rogers seemed to notice that something was happening. "Ah, Dean Elmore," he said. "Perhaps it *is*

a bit premature to speculate on what the board might do."
He sneaked a quick upward glance at Coach Thomas.

Thomas was not mollified. He reached out for Elmore.

What happened next was seen by both Burns and Mal
Tomlin, who had crushed his cigarette in his plate and was
now watching with as much interest as Burns. Elmore attempted to scoot his chair backward, but because he did not
rise from it, it was difficult to move on the rug on the dining
room floor. When Thomas's hand had almost reached him,
Elmore made one more attempt to scoot out of harm's way,
this time giving a good backward push. He gave too good a
push, or so it seemed to Burns, and toppled his chair over.
Coach Thomas looked as surprised as anyone to see Elmore
on the rug, his chair half on top of him, scuttling around like
a pair of ragged claws, trying to get out from under his chair,
trying to escape from Thomas, trying to regain a little of his
dignity.

Coach Thomas reached down a hand to help Elmore to
his feet, but Elmore, fearing violence, or maybe fearing as-
sistance, scuttled backward. He finally got to his feet and
continued backward until he hit the wall.

Burns looked at Mal Tomlin, who appeared about to
strangle, his laughter making spasmodic efforts to force its
way past his tightly shut lips. Burns grabbed Tomlin's
shoulder and dragged him from the table, both of them
making their way to the door and going out. Burns hoped
that Elmore hadn't seen them. God only knew what he would
do to punish any witnesses to what had happened.

Once they were outside, Mal Tomlin broke into guffaws
of laughter. Burns joined him. Coach Thomas emerged right
behind them. His face was much more serious, and Burns
and Tomlin soon calmed down, though Tomlin had more
trouble controlling himself than Burns.

"He's threatening to sue me," Thomas said. "Says I shoved
him down and tried to beat him up. I didn't do it." Thomas
had a puzzled look, as if he couldn't quite figure out what

22

was going on. It was a look that Burns had seen often on the faces of people who had dealings with Elmore.

"Don't worry, Coach," Burns said. "Mal and I saw it all. We'll be your witnesses. Rogers saw it too."

Mal Tomlin shook out a cigarette and lit it, not an easy job, considering the wind velocity. He put his disposable lighter back in his pocket and said, "I wouldn't count too much on Rogers. He's never contradicted Elmore before."

"It's still the three of us against the two of them," Burns said. "Elmore will realize that. He'll never sue anybody, Coach. He's just a bully, and he likes to make threats."

The coach seemed to relax a little. "I guess you're right," he said. "Still . . . I didn't even touch him."

"We know," Tomlin said. "Go on home and enjoy the weekend. He'll have forgotten all about it by Monday."

"Okay, thanks," Thomas said. "I'll do that. I've got worse things to worry about, after all." He turned away and started toward the Gymnasium (Hartley Gorman VI).

"He's right," Burns said. "If the board does approve dropping the sports program, he'll be out of a job."

"They'll keep him on," Tomlin said. "They'll just cut his salary."

"Maybe so, but I'd hate to be the one to tell the players," Burns said.

"Me, too. I think I'll take my own advice and go home," Tomlin said. "See you Monday."

"Sure," Burns said. "See you Monday." He started back to Main, where his car was parked, thinking about Monday.

Burns's car, which he intended to keep forever, or as long as was humanly possible, was a 1967 Plymouth Fury III, the kind they didn't make any more, a gas gobbler from the word go, in which eight adults could ride in comfort. Its only real drawback was the vinyl seats, which were hot in summer and, as they were now, cold in winter. But the car started immediately, and the heater would be warm in a minute. Burns headed for home.

"Home" was three miles from the school in a nondescript tract house amid a hundred other tract houses built at a time when Pecan City had been going through a minor period of growth. Burns had gotten the house cheap, the previous owners having been transferred to another area and in dire need of capital. It was basic housing, and it suited Burns just fine. He knew his neighbors barely well enough to speak to, and he lived quietly in anonymous bachelorhood.

Once inside, Burns poured himself a glass of grape juice, put a couple of Creedence Clearwater LPs on the turntable, and sat on the couch reading a new Hemingway biography. He found it difficult to concentrate on the book, however; thoughts of Elmore kept intruding.

Elmore had always been Elmore, as far as Burns knew. He had been on the campus for several years before Burns had arrived and had already managed to alienate everyone who came in contact with him. At that time, though, he had been in the relatively harmless position of teaching biology. He had been filled even then with mad plans for the improvement of the school, but no one had taken him seriously, not even when he stood up in faculty meetings to explain his plans to the assembled multitude. When the position of academic dean had come open three years before, owing to the untimely demise of Dean Clark—a wise, respected, and even loved man—most people who knew that Elmore had applied for the job laughed openly. Most of them were now working elsewhere, and there was Elmore, dean indeed.

No one was quite sure how it had happened. It was now harder to find a member of the selection committee who would admit voting for him than it was to find a registered voter who would admit that he voted for Richard Nixon in 1968. Apparently Rogers had taken a hand in things behind the scenes, but that, too, was kept very quiet. Maybe, thought Burns, Elmore really *did* have the goods on someone.

Unable to read, Burns put down his book and went into

the room he liked to call his library. Built-in shelves lined the walls of the room intended by the builder as a dining area. All the shelves were filled with books, not necessarily books that Burns would have wanted his students and colleagues to know that he read—mysteries, science fiction, horror, popular fiction of every stripe. It was Burns's opinion that even an English teacher couldn't read Faulkner all the time.

In the middle of the room was a dilapidated desk, a far cry from the one Burns had at school. Burns sat down at the desk in a straight-backed wooden chair and opened the top drawer. Several sheets of paper were stacked neatly inside. Burns took out the top one and looked at the heading: *The Ten Best Bad Movies of All Time*. It was a list that had bothered him a little because it had two Viking movies on it, *The Long Ships* and *The Vikings*. He wasn't quite sure it was fair to have two movies with the same sort of subject matter on such a short list. He looked at the list for almost five minutes. Then he drew a line through *The Vikings*. It took him most of the rest of the afternoon to decide to replace it with *The Black Shield of Falworth*.

Burns liked to get to his office early. He liked to arrive at least an hour before classes began at eight o'clock so that he could read his newspaper, organize his thoughts, plan his day, or just generally goof around the office. He wasn't one of those people who could drive into the parking lot at three minutes before the beginning of class, jog up the three flights of stairs, and begin lecturing.

On Monday, however, he didn't even get to finish his paper. Bunni walked into the office at seven-twenty. Right behind her was her boyfriend, George ("The Ghost") Kaspar. George was a good example of what was wrong with Coach Thomas's football team. He was five-eleven, fairly stocky, and weighed about one-eighty. Maybe one-ninety with all his gear on, suited up for the game. And George was the largest of Coach Thomas's defensive tackles. Even the

25

strong of stomach had to look away at times when the HGC Panthers attempted a pass rush. It often appeared that opposing passers had time to get a haircut and a manicure while looking for a receiver; it appeared that way because such was often the case.

None of which was Coach Thomas's fault, really. It isn't easy to recruit the cream of the crop to play football at a tiny denominational school a hundred miles from the nearest major population center. Thomas had to take whatever was left over after the Southwest Conference and the larger schools got through.

George had been in Burns's American literature class the previous spring. He had been no genius, but he had tried hard and done fairly well. Burns liked him.

"I hope it's all right if we come in and talk to you," Bunni said.

Burns put down his newspaper and took his feet off the desk. "Sure," he said. "Have a seat."

Bunni and George sat.

"What can I do for you?" Burns asked. He had a pretty good idea what they wanted. Department heads were supposed to keep what transpired at the Friday meetings to themselves, but someone always talked, much to the chagrin of Dean Elmore, who had done everything but put a "Loose Lips Sink Ships" poster up in the faculty dining room.

Bunni and George looked at each other. "We've heard a rumor," Bunni said, apparently having been chosen as the spokesperson.

"That's not unusual around here," Burns said, truthfully enough. Rumors at HGC were as common as prayer meetings. They had grown especially rife since Elmore had become dean.

"This is a rumor about the sports program," Bunni said.

"So what's the rumor?" Burns asked.

"That there won't *be* a sports program," Bunni said. Her eyes were wide with the enormity of it all. "That football and basketball and . . . and *every*thing will just be . . . gone!"

"You can't be sure about rumors like that," Burns said, feeling like a slimy worm. "Something like that couldn't happen just over the weekend. Something like that would take board approval." He stopped. He didn't know what else to say.

George decided it was time to speak up. "We heard that Dean Elmore is going to take the idea to the board and tell them that the school can save a lot of money if we do away with sports."

The kid had a pretty good source of information, Burns had to admit. "Taking it to them and getting their approval are two different things," he said. "I imagine some of the board members are old football players themselves, and most of them probably like coming to the homecoming games. Elmore won't have an easy time of it. Assuming, of course, that what you heard is true."

"It's true, all right," Bunni said. She clenched her fists on her nicely rounded thighs. "I really do hate that Dean Elmore."

Burns was surprised. He'd certainly never seen Bunni express so much emotion before, not even when they'd discussed Jonathan Edwards's "Sinners in the Hands of an Angry God" in the American literature class.

"Is there anything we can do, Dr. Burns?" George asked.

Burns sat silently for a minute. If he did anything at all to help these students, he would get in serious trouble if Elmore found out. But what the hell. "Write this down, Bunni, he said. "I'm going to give you a list."

Burns and Earl Fox were sitting in the history lounge, smoking L & Ms, when Dorinda Edgely opened the door and walked in.

She looked like a pig.

It wasn't her figure, though the orange and black polyester pants she wore, and probably had been wearing since abouι

27

1974, were stuffed to the bursting point with her bountiful self.

It wasn't the fact that her blonde hair seemed to have been styled by the very man who created Miss Piggy's "do" for "The Muppets."

It wasn't the rosy pinkness of the flesh of her chubby face and double chins.

No, it was none of those things.

It was the snout.

Dorinda Edgely was wearing a snout, which would have been right at home on the Practical Pig in the Disney cartoon. It was pink and wrinkled, and it had two black nostrils painted on. It was attached to Dorinda's face by a thin black stretch band, like the kind that Burns had once used on Halloween to hold his Lone Ranger mask.

Around Dorinda's neck was a piece of white string, from which a sign was hanging. The sign said HELP ME KISS A PIG in purple block letters.

Dorinda held a tin can from which the label had been removed. She rattled it at Burns and Fox. Burns could hear the sound of coins clattering around inside the can. He took a deep drag on his cigarette and blew out a puff of smoke.

Fox, meanwhile, had dropped his cigarette to the floor as soon as the door had begun to open. It had rolled aside a few feet, and Fox completely ignored the fact that it was there at all, even though it was sending up a steady stream of smoke. "Hi, Dorinda," he said. "You're looking great!"

Dorinda stopped shaking the can.

"I mean, you've got on a great get-up! Doesn't she Carl? Isn't that great? It's great! What's it for?"

"The contest," Dorinda said. "Surely you're aware of the contest?"

"Oh, sure!" Fox said. "The contest. We know about the contest, don't we, Carl?"

As a matter of fact, Burns *did* know about the contest. Every year a member of the faculty got to kiss a pig in the student dining room at noon on a Thursday. For this privilege, the faculty member had to raise more money than any other faculty member entered in the contest. Though the money went to a scholarship fund, Burns had always declined the honor of entering. Kissing a pig in front of the students was not his idea of a good time.

"Sure," Burns said. "We know about the contest. How much money have you collected, Dorinda?"

"I haven't counted it," she said. "But I hope to have a little more when I get out of here." She looked pointedly at the cigarette burning on the floor.

"Absolutely!" Fox said, fumbling in the back pocket of his faded bell-bottom jeans for his billfold. He pulled it out, looked inside, and extracted a wrinkled dollar bill. "Here," he said, extending it toward Dorinda.

Dorinda took the bill and looked expectantly at Burns, who took another defiant drag on his L & M. "Is Dean Elmore entered this year?" he asked.

"Why?" Dorinda countered.

"Don't worry," Burns said. "I'm going to give my money to you, not to him. I was just wondering."

"All right then," Dorinda said. "He's entered. He beat me last year, but I plan to beat him this year." She held her can out toward Burns.

Burns dug in his pocket for some change and came up with two quarters and a penny. He dropped them in the can. "Good luck, Dorinda. I really hope you win."

"Thanks," she said. Having gotten what she came for, she left the history lounge, not even bothering to shut the door.

Burns got up and closed the door himself, giving Fox time to step on his still-smoldering cigarette butt. "You've got to get a lock for this thing," Burns said.

"That woman has no respect," Fox said. "All I can say is that I feel sorry for the pig if she wins."

"And what if Elmore wins?"

"Then the SPCA will descend on us in all its fury, and

rightfully so," Fox said. "Because the pig would probably die instantly. Can you believe what he did to Thomas last Friday?"

"After a few years at this place, I'm no longer surprised by anything at all," Burns said, "but that did seem particularly brutal." He dropped his butt into the Diet Coke can, which by now was beginning to get quite full. "Time to get a new ashtray. And speaking of last Friday, has anyone been called in for a conference with Elmore? I'm interested to find out what his 'secret plan' is."

"Ah," Fox said, reaching for the L & M pack. "I've been waiting for you to ask. I had my conference this morning. I expect that you'll be called in pretty soon. I know the whole thing, and I think it just may be the one thing that will surprise you, even after all these years."

"So tell me."

Fox lit the cigarette and took a drag. "Well," he said, "it's like this . . ."

4

ELMORE'S "SECRET PLAN," which was of course no longer a secret, was simple and direct: he was going to turn Hartley Gorman College into a degree mill. Or at least that's what it amounted to. The school would begin to award credit hours for "undirected study" by "independent scholars."

"Now what *that* means," Fox said, leaning forward and scattering ashes across the top of the card table, "is that let's say you'd read a couple hundred books on American history. You'd know a lot about history if you'd retained any of what you read, maybe even more than the average college student, who, after all, reads just *one* book. So surely you'd deserve some college credit for your work if you asked for it, wouldn't you? Especially if you were ready and able to *pay* for it?" Every time he emphasized a word, Fox would wave his hand and send more ashes flying.

"Good Lord," Burns said. It was all he could think of.

"It's not that simple, of course," Fox said. "Can't make it *too* easy, or someone might think we weren't being rigorous enough. So we department heads—that's you and me, buddy—will have to interview the 'independent scholars' to find out how much they know. You can bet that Elmore will be right in there when it comes to deciding the guidelines for the interviews, and that it won't be easy to fail one. I can just imagine the questions in history. 'Who was our first president?' 'Who was known as the Great Emancipator?' Things like that." He paused for a second. "Come to thing of it, maybe the second one's too hard. But you get the idea."

"Yeah," Burns said. "I get the idea."

31

"Well," asked Fox, "are you surprised?"

Burns thought about it. "I have to admit it," he said. "I'm surprised. I never thought I would be, but I am. Doesn't Elmore realize that if he pushes something like this through, the regular degree will be cheapened so much that it'll be almost worthless?"

Fox laughed. "I don't think he cares. Think how much money he can bring in from people who want a degree but who don't want to have to go to school. And it's all perfectly legal."

"Are you sure?"

"Sure I'm sure. He'll even tell you the name of the congressional act when he talks to you. The act that makes it legal, I mean. *Ethical* I'm not sure about, but legally he's on solid ground."

"This is really going to infuriate a lot of old-timers around here," Burns said. "Do you think we'll get a vote on it?"

"You, of all people, should recall what Clem and the Curriculum Committee went through a few years back, and the executive decision that came out of that," Fox said. "Elmore may present this to the faculty, but you don't have to worry about our getting a vote on it."

They sat there at the decrepit card table, thinking about working for a degree mill, until the bell rang. "Let's get lunch," Burns said. "How about Chinese?"

"Fine by me," Fox said. "Let's go by for Mal."

They got up and went into the hall, which was clogged with students. There were stairways at either end of the hall, but no one was making any progress in going down. Two students stood at the head of the stairs, and each student was holding a clipboard. Students would sign something on the clipboard and then be allowed to go on down. The usual hum of between-class activity was amplified about five times by the crowding.

"What the heck is going on?" Fox asked.

Burns didn't know for sure, but he could make a pretty

good guess. "I suspect it's a petition," he said.

"A petition?"

"If I were guessing," Burns said, "which of course I am, I'd guess that it was a petition making some statement about the importance of athletics to the students here and maybe saying something about the necessity of continuing to have a competitive athletic program to promote school and community spirit."

Fox looked at him suspiciously. "Did you have anything to do with this?"

Burns looked innocent. He actually hadn't thought Bunni could get things organized so quickly. "Not me," he said. "I'm sure this is a purely student-generated petition."

"I'll bet," Fox said. "Well, let's go back in the lounge and have another smoke. We're not going to get down those stairs for a few minutes, that's for sure."

After lunch, Burns, Tomlin, and Fox drove back via the Administration Building (Hartley Gorman II) at Burns's insistence. This was the second-oldest building on the campus, squat and ugly, but solidly constructed of serviceable red brick. There was a rose garden in front, filled at this time of the year with dry stalks rasping against one another.

Today, however, there was something added. In front of the building, nine or ten students carrying posters were marching up and down. The posters were painted in the school colors and said things like FOOTBALL FOREVER, PANTHER PRIDE, WINNERS NEVER QUIT, and WE SHALL OVERCOME. Off to one side, several members of the Panther Marching Band were playing the school fight song.

Mal Tomlin, who had been conned into driving, slowed almost to a stop, which was a good thing. He was laughing so hard that he might otherwise have been the cause of a serious wreck. " 'We shall overcome'?" he yelled, gasping for breath between laughs. " 'We shall overcome'?"

"It's the thought that counts," Burns said, laughing as well.

"What next?" Fox wondered.

Burns calmed down. "If I were guessing," he said, "which of course I am, I'd say that there might be a huge spontaneous pep rally in front of the women's dorm about seven o'clock tonight, after which all the little rallyers will probably march down to that vacant field at the end of the street here"—he gestured behind them with his thumb—"and then there'll be a big spontaneous bonfire, all in support of athletics at HGC."

Fox looked at him sharply. "I know damn well you had something to do with all this."

"Not me," Burns said. "All I did was make a little list."

"I don't care whose idea it was," Tomlin said, recovering himself and driving on. "I bet our pal Elmore is sitting in there having a stroke right about now."

"I sincerely hope so," Burns said.

When Burns climbed back to the third floor of Main to keep his afternoon office hours, he was greeted by a sign taped to the wall near the classroom at the head of the stairs. Printed with black Magic Marker on college-ruled notebook paper, the sign said:

> PLEAse!
> Do not !!
> LEAve cANs!
> UnDeR Desk!!!
>   MAiD Rose

Rose was the black woman who cleaned the building. No one referred to her as the "maid," but she always signed her notes with that title. Her notes were famous throughout the building, and they were always couched in strong language and heavy with exclamation marks. Rose had her own ideas about how the building should be run, and she didn't tolerate any deviation. What this particular note meant was that

34

someone, probably Burns, had been lax in enforcing the school's rule against soft-drink cans in the classroom, and Rose was chapped.

Since Rose was built along the lines a defensive lineman should be built, rather than like the relatively skinny George ("The Ghost") Kaspar, Burns always tried to go along with her demands. He would have to be more careful in policing his classroom. Actually, few of the students who brought the cans into the room were drinking the contents. The cans had already been emptied, and were being used as spittoons. Snuff-dipping was a common habit at HGC, and some of Rose's more dramatic notes had been composed on the days she found snuff that had been spit into the trash cans.

Burns took down the sign, as he always did, and went on to his office. Almost as soon as hc got to his desk and sat down, Clem and Miss Darling appeared at his door. Clem's color was high, and Miss Darling was fairly jumping up and down. They've heard, Burns thought.

"Dr. Burns. Dr. Burns," Miss Darling said in her high, breathy voice. "Oh, Dr. Burns. Do you . . . Have you . . . Is it true . . ."

Burns hadn't seen Miss Darling so upset since one of her students had ridiculed a Walt Whitman poem and called the author "an old fairy." It had taken him all afternoon to get her calmed down after he finally got a coherent story out of her.

Clem helped out this time in her usual straightforward way. "What we would like to know," she said, "is whether it's true that Dean Elmore plans to turn HGC into a degree mill."

Nothing traveled faster than a campus rumor, Burns thought. What he didn't understand was why Miss Darling was so exercised. Nothing that Elmore had ever done in the past had bothered her. He didn't ask, though. He simply said, "Not exactly."

"And what does 'not exactly' mean?" Clem asked.

35

"It means 'not exactly,' " Burns said. "Why don't you two have a seat."

They sat. Clem, as usual, looked composed in her brown outfit, severely tailored to fit her compact frame. Miss Darling, also as usual, looked dithery. She was a short, doll-like woman, who always wore frilly blouses and full skirts. Her hair was tightly curled and of an indeterminate mousy brown color that varied at the whim of her hairdresser. She wore too much make-up, in contrast to Clem, who wore hardly any, and her cheeks were always fiery red.

After he had organized his thoughts, Burns said, "Now, let me tell you one thing straight off. I haven't talked to Dean Elmore myself. I assume that he will get to me fairly soon. So I know only what I've heard through the rumor mill—just like you two, I suspect."

"And you've heard . . . you know that . . . they say that . . . " Miss Darling dithered.

". . . about this degree mill business," Clem finished for her.

Burns told them what he knew.

"That's despicable," Clem said.

"Yes," said Miss Darling. "It's . . . well, it's just . . . I mean to say that . . ." She trailed off into silence.

"It may not be as bad as it sounds," Burns said. "It's all perfectly legal, and I'm sure Dean Elmore intends to explain the whole thing to the faculty in a general meeting."

"Carl Burns, you're beginning to sound as if you agree with the whole thing. Next you'll be telling us how much you love the humanities course!" Clem was in her severe mode, and Carl would have been terrified had he been a freshman student. As it was, he was a little uncomfortable.

"I'm just trying to withhold judgment," he said. "As it stands, you're right. It stinks on ice."

"Oh, dear," Miss Darling said. "Oh, dear." She shook her head, got out of the chair, and toddled off to her office.

"I've never seen her get so upset," Burns said. "At least

not recently. How did you hear?"

"Never mind how we heard," Clem said. "It's no wonder the poor woman is upset. Why, she's taught here for nearly forty years. She's seen a lot of things in her time, but this has to be the worst."

"But surely—," Burns began, but Clem cut him off.

"Don't surely me," she said. "I know what you think. You think she won't remember any of this tomorrow, and you're probably right. But the reputation of this school means something to her, and this time Elmore is going to destroy exactly that—the school's reputation."

Everyone at HGC was convinced that Elmore had spies among the faculty, people who pretended to disagree with his policies but who reported every derogatory remark directly to him. Burns knew that Clem was not one of these spies, though he believed that they existed. Abner Swan, for instance, was a spy if ever there was one. But Burns knew that he could trust Clem, just as he trusted Mal Tomlin and Earl Fox. So he said, "You're right, of course, but we can't do anything about it right now."

"And why not?" Clem said. "Tell me that. Why not? This time Elmore's gone too far. He's gone over the edge, if you ask me. Someone has got to do something to stop him."

Burns though about it. This wasn't something like the sports program, something that you could rally the whole student body to protest. Most of the students wouldn't care. And you couldn't rally the faculty, either.

"Look, Clem," Burns said, "if we tried something like a protest, or even a petition, no one would help. Everyone here's too scared that he's going to lose his job. If we get to vote on this in a faculty meeting, or even if it's just brought up for discussion, I promise you that I'll speak out against it, but you and I both know that no one else will."

"I will," Clem said.

"You know what I mean," Burns said. "I will, you will, maybe even one or two others will, but that's all. Then Elmore will take a vote by a show of hands, if he takes a vote at all, and we'll lose. That's just the way it is."

"I don't believe it," Clem said.

"Believe it," Burns said.

"No. I won't. This time, I'm not going to let Elmore get the better of me." Clem stood up. "This time, I'm going to beat him."

"I hope you're right," Burns said.

"I am. You'll see." She turned and walked out of the office.

Burns waited for a few minutes, but no other faculty members came by to discuss the rumor. He opened his middle drawer and took out his list of things he hated, but he couldn't get interested in it. So he spent the rest of the afternoon rereading *The Sun Also Rises*. He was interrupted only once, by a call from Dean Elmore's secretary, asking him to stop by the Dean's office on Tuesday at eleven-fifteen. He said that he would be there.

5

BURNS WAS FIVE minutes late for his appointment. Had he been there on time, he might have seen the killer. He might even have prevented the murder. As it was, he found the body.

As Burns left Main through the rear door, the Administration Building was to his left and slightly closer to the street. He met no one on his way there, which was not unusual considering the day and the hour. Every Tuesday and Thursday at eleven, HGC had assembly, formerly known as Chapel. Elmore had changed the name because so many of the programs were not of a religious nature that "Chapel" no longer seemed appropriate. It was one of the few decisions made by the dean with which Burns agreed.

Attendance at assembly was compulsory for students, though not for faculty. Burns seldom attended. In fact, few faculty members did. Abner Swan always did, of course, and he encouraged his faculty to go, but most of them were like Burns and went only when the program appeared to be especially interesting.

Burns entered the Administration Building and climbed the stairs to the second floor. An elevator had been installed several years earlier, but Burns was so used to the stairs in Main that he never used it.

At the top of the stairs Burns turned right and walked down a carpeted hall to the offices. On the right was President Rogers's office, but there was no one visible inside. Both Rogers and his secretary usually went to assembly, where Rogers nearly always introduced the program or made some remarks.

There was no one in Elmore's outer office, either. His secretary was no doubt attending assembly with most of the others in the building. The administration liked to keep up appearances, and they expected their secretaries to do likewise.

In fact, it was unusual for Dean Elmore to conduct business during a scheduled assembly period, but, as Burns suddenly recalled, today was Football Awards Day, a traditional event at the end of the season, even at the end of such miserable seasons as HGC had been having lately. So Elmore probably felt that he didn't need to lend his presence to anything that supported the athletic program. The only thing out of character was that Elmore hadn't gone to ridicule the coach and make fun of the team's losing record.

Burns hesitated for a minute in the secretary's office. He could hear no sound from the inner room, but he assumed that Elmore must be in there. He stepped to the open door and raised his hand to knock, at the same time glancing around the wainscoting to see if Elmore was at his desk.

He was there, all right, but not exactly in the position that Burns had expected to find him. His upper body had fallen across the top of his desk, his arms outstretched as if he were reaching for something that was slipping off the opposite side. His head was turned to face the open door, and his mouth was slackly open. A thin line of blood trailed from between his lips. His open eyes stared blankly in Burns's direction.

At first, Burns thought that Elmore had perhaps had a stroke or a heart attack—the man was a Type "A" if ever there was one—but then he noticed the large bruise in the vicinity of Elmore's temple. Within the area covered by the bruise there was a sizeable dent, no doubt caused by some heavy object's having been used to bash Elmore in the head.

Burns stood in the door for a few minutes, or seconds, he

40

was never sure which, contemplating Elmore's body. He didn't know whether to go in and take a pulse or to call the police. He knew from his reading that he shouldn't touch anything, so he decided that the call to the police was best. Before he turned to make the call, he noticed one last detail. Under Elmore's head, protruding slightly and crushed but still recognizable, was a pink pig's snout made of cardboard.

"Boss" Napier, chief of Pecan City's police force, attended the on-site investigation himself and immediately announced his intention of taking a leading part in apprehending the perpetrator. It was an election year, after all, and Napier was expecting heavy opposition from a man who disapproved of Napier's methods and who cited figures to show that crime in Pecan City was on the rise. Napier must have decided that the pig snout was a hot clue and that the perpetrator would be brought to book in short order.

Napier was a fine figure of a man, who looked like a police chief should look. He was a bit over six feet tall, beefy and blonde, and usually wore, as he did today, jeans, a western-style shirt (this one was blue, with white and red flowers on it), boots, and a brown leather jacket.

Napier had arrived with his homicide team shortly after Burns's call, just in time to isolate Elmore's office before everyone returned from assembly. The outer office door was now secured with a yellow ribbon with the words CRIME SCENE KEEP OUT printed on it in black. An officer was posted along with it in case anyone got too curious. Burns had been hustled down the hall to a small storage room containing, along with buckets, mops, and brooms, a small table and chair. It was a lot like the history lounge.

The door was closed and Napier was questioning Burns, who could hear the noise of confusion and discussion in the hall beyond. There was no bereavement, however, and Burns didn't really expect any. In fact, he expected unbridled joy as soon as the word got out, if not dancing in the streets.

41

The denomination didn't approve of dancing.

Burns was sitting in the chair. Napier was standing. "So," he said, fixing Burns with a glare from his ice-blue eyes, "who do you know that might have a motive for killing Dean Delmar?"

"That's *Elmore*," Burns said. He wished that Fox were there with an L & M.

"Whatever," Napier said with a shrug. "Somebody didn't like him enough and bashed him in the head. Any ideas?" Obviously his assessment of the situation agreed with Burns's.

"It could have been anybody," Burns said.

"I know that," Napier said. "I want some names."

"Get a copy of the college catalog," Burns said. "It has a list of all the faculty members."

Napier took a menacing step forward. "Nobody likes a smart ass, Barnes."

"That's *Burns*."

Napier leaned forward and put his palms on the table. "I could skin your sorry ass right here in this room and hang your hide out to dry," he said. "Maybe you did it."

Burns tried to speak, cleared his throat, then tried again. "You don't understand," he croaked. He could never recall having been threatened in his entire life.

"Damned right, I don't understand," Napier said. "I don't understand why a sorry-ass guy like you tries to make funny remarks. You aren't in a funny situation."

Burns had heard all sorts of rumors about how Napier had gotten his nickname. One was that he had developed a secret wrestling hold, akin to the notorious Von Erich "Iron Claw," which he used on recalcitrant prisoners—those he was sure had committed the crimes to which they refused to confess. The hold left no marks and caused permanent brain damage. It was also noised about that during deer season, Napier would retreat to a desolate lodge on a secluded hunting lease armed only with a bull whip and a .357 magnum. What he did

42

there and to what or to whom he did it was supposedly too horrible to contemplate.

Oddly enough, in spite of the rumors and in spite of the fact that he had originally been intimidated, Burns found that he was not scared at all. "I'm not trying to be funny," he said. "It's just that . . . have you ever seen that movie, *Murder on the Orient Express*?"

Napier gave a light push with his forearms and stood upright again. "Movies? You're giving me movies now?"

"Let me explain, please," Burns said.

"I wish you would."

"Look," Burns said. "I'm trying. But you keep interrupting. Can't you just drop the intimidation routine for a minute?"

Napier looked shocked, but he said, "Okay. Tell it your way. But get on with it."

"You've probably seen the movie," Burns said. "It's been on television. It's the one where—"

"Wait a minute," Napier said. "Is that James Bond guy in it? Only without his rug on? What's his name? Donnelly?"

"Sean Connery," Burns said. "Yes. He's in it. In the end . . ."

"Okay," Napier said. "I see what you mean. You think everybody in the school catalog had a hand in this business?"

"Of course not," Burns said. "But I expect that everybody in there had a motive. Dean Elmore was not universally loved and respected."

"Nobody liked him, huh?"

"Nobody. Well, President Rogers didn't seem to mind him, but aside from him—"

"—nobody."

"Right."

"Including you."

"Including me," Burns said. "But I was the one who called you, remember?"

Napier smiled, but it wasn't a pleasant smile. It was more of a predatory smile. "Doesn't mean a thing," he said. "But we can get back to you later. Right now let's test out your powers of observation. You were the first one on the scene, so you say. If that's so, where's the murder weapon?"

"I didn't take it, if that's what you mean," Burns said.

Napier walked over to the table, hiked up his left leg, and parked his buttocks on the table's edge. "If you didn't take it, then where is it?" he inquired mildly.

Burns didn't know, but it was something he'd thought about. He'd seen nothing on the desk that could have been used to cosh in Elmore's head. "Maybe there's something on the floor, or under the desk," he said. "Your team in there ought to find it."

"Maybe, maybe not. You visit DeLore's office often?"

"That's Elmore. Not often. Why?"

"Just wondered if you noticed anything missing off the desk, Napier said.

"Oh." Burns thought about it. The photo of Elmore's son, Wayne, a prissy senior derisively and openly referred to by the other students as "Little Dean," had been there, as it always was. So had the black plastic "IN" and "OUT" baskets with one or two manila campus-mail envelopes in them. And the "Success Desk Calendar" and the HGC pen and pencil set from the school bookstore. And the beige telephone. And the . . .

"Paper clips," Burns said.

"He wasn't killed by any paper clips," Napier said.

"No, no," Burns said. "He had a sort of cut-glass paper-clip holder on his desk. I remember getting a paper-clip out of it one time when I was in there. I don't think I saw it today."

Napier got off the table and went out of the room. In a minute, he was back. "You're pretty good," he said. "It's not there, and it wasn't on the floor, either. How big was this thing?"

Burns made a shape with his hands. "About like this," he said, "about the size of a softball." He thought for a minute. "If it *was* cut glass, I imagine it was pretty heavy."

44

"And now it's gone," Napier said. "That's mighty interesting, wouldn't you say?"

"I suppose so," Burns said.

"Yeah, well, maybe he loaned it to a friend. We'll see." Napier came and sat on the edge of the table again, one foot touching the floor. "Since you're so smart, what do you make of that pig's snout?"

"I . . . I'm not sure what you mean."

"Sure you're sure. I mean just what I said. You think that snout's a comment? On Elmond, I mean. It's us cops that're usually called pigs, but from what you say about this guy, well, maybe somebody thought *he* was a pig."

"Elmore," Burns said.

"Whatever," Napier said. "You ever see that snout before?"

"I don't know," Burns said, which was true. He wasn't going to say anything that he wasn't absolutely sure of.

Napier wasn't stupid, despite his difficulty with names. "You ever see a snout that *looked like* that one?"

Burns thought about Dorinda Edgely. "I can't be sure," he said.

Napier leaned close to him, and Burns twisted in his chair. "Look, Binz, don't play your intellectual English teacher's word games with me. Tell me about that snout."

"Burns," Burns said. "And I really can't be sure. I didn't stay around in Elmore's office to examine things. I saw the snout sticking out from under his head, yes, but I didn't take the time to give it a thorough going-over."

"A snout's a snout," Napier said. "Cut the crap."

"All right," Burns said. He told Napier about the Kiss a Pig contest. "Dorinda Edgely was wearing a snout like that one, but that was yesterday. And it may not have been the same one."

"Leave the detecting to me," Napier said. "Tell me about this Edgely."

Burns didn't have much to tell. Dorinda Edgely had joined

the Psychology Department five or six years before—he wasn't sure, but that could be checked easily enough. Since Elmore's deanship, she had in fact been one of his few supporters, except when it came to kissing the pig. "She just couldn't have killed him," Burns said. "I think she actually *liked* the man. At faculty functions, she was about the only one who'd even talk to him."

"Any hanky-panky going on there?" Napier asked.

Burns almost laughed. "Hardly," he said. "Elmore's wife has been dead for several years, but he'd never be stupid enough to fool around with a faculty member."

As soon as he said it, however, Burns began to wonder. Dorinda, stretching her years' old polyester to the limit, with her obviously touched-up curls, might be just the sort to appeal to Elmore. He wondered . . .

"Well, we'll find out," Napier said. "I think that's all for you right now, Baines, but don't go out of town. I'm still not sure about you."

"That's Burns. And I won't be going anywhere. I've got classes to teach."

"Fine," Napier said. "Go teach a few of 'em."

Burns got out the chair and left.

6

THE WIND PLUCKED at Burns's jacket as he walked back to Main, and when he arrived he was not surprised to see a sign attached to the door with transparent tape:

PLEASE!
CLOSE!!
The DOOR!!
HiGH WinD!!!
MAiD Rose

On days when the wind was from the north, it sometimes whipped right down the main hall and stripped all the announcements right off the bulletin boards. Burns made sure he tugged the door shut against the draft.

Mal Tomlin was waiting right inside. "Elmore's dead, right?"

Burns nodded.

"Hot damn. Who did it?" Tomlin reached inside his jacket. "Want a cigarette?"

"Yes," said Burns. "Or two. Let's go upstairs."

They headed up to the history lounge. Earl Fox was waiting for them. He had his Cowboys windbreaker on. "Come on in and close the door," he said. "I've got to hear this."

As soon as all three had cigarettes going, Burns told them what had happened.

"So you found the body?" Tomlin said.

"That's right."

"Ah, I suppose that you didn't . . . ah . . ."

Burns tapped ash into a Diet Pepsi can which had replaced the Diet Coke can. "Don't even say it," he said.

"It was just a thought," Tomlin said. "What did you tell the cops?"

"Not much," Burns said. "I didn't know much. Boss Napier wanted to know who I thought might have done it."

"God," Fox said. "It'd be a lot easier to tell him who might *not* have done it." He tried to blow a smoke ring and failed. "In fact, he might be getting quite a few confessions. Whoever did it will be a hero."

"Are there any clues?" Tomlin asked.

Burns didn't know what to say. Napier hadn't told him not to discuss things, but he still didn't feel right about revealing information. On the other hand, anything he said would probably be easily found out by reading the next day's edition of the *Pecan City News-Advertiser*. So he told them about the snout.

"Was it the one Dorinda was wearing the other day?" Fox asked.

"I don't have any idea," Burns said. "Of course it *looked* like the same one, but that doesn't mean anything. I'm leaving all that to the cops."

"Who do you think Rogers will appoint to be acting dean?" Fox asked.

No one had thought about that. "I just hope it's not me," Tomlin said. "I've got enough grief. Say—you don't think someone knocked him off to get the job, do you?"

"Stranger things have happened," Burns said. He dropped his cigarette butt into the Pepsi can, where it made a satisfactory hiss in the remains of the NutraSweetened cola. "What I wonder is how this will affect the plans Elmore had for the athletic program and for turning this place into a degree mill."

"Damn," Tomlin said. "You don't think Coach Thomas . . ."

48

"I don't think anything," Burns said. "Except that it's time for me to go up and keep a few office hours and then go home."

"Business as usual, huh?" Fox said.

"As much as possible," Burns said, getting up. "As much as possible."

Tomlin got up too. "I guess you're right, kid. Watch out for that pigeon shit, though." He slapped Burns on the shoulder, and both of them left. Fox lit another cigarette.

Burns never locked his office during the day. He never even closed the door. Students at HGC seemed for the most part to respect his property and the privacy of his office; he'd never had anything stolen. On occasion, however, he'd returned to his office to find someone sitting in a chair and waiting for him. Today it was Don Elliott.

The little speech and drama chairman was an interesting contradiction. He was barely over five feet tall and looked as if he'd just come off a long hunger strike, yet he had an impressively booming baritone voice, which could be heard without amplification from the stage to the farthest seats in the highest balcony of any auditorium. And in spite of his size, he was one of the most impressive trenchermen Burns had ever seen. At the Friday luncheons, he often seemed to stagger beneath the weight of his loaded plate; and the way he could stack meat, vegetables, various salads, and bread to incredible heights and still make it to the table without spilling a thing was a wonder of balance and coordination.

"Hello, Burns," Elliott said in what passed for a whisper with him. "I hope you don't mind my intrusion. I would like to talk with you, if I may."

"Of course," Burns said, crossing between Elliott and his desk. "What's up?" Gaining his chair, Burns sat down.

"May I close the door?"

Burns wasn't sure where this was leading, but he said, "All right."

49

Elliott got up, closed the door quietly, and returned to the chair. "Two things," he said. Then he waited.

"Fine," Burns finally said.

"In confidence, I hope," Elliott said.

"Naturally," Burns said, still having no idea what was going on.

"Good," Elliott said, leaning forward slightly and almost causing Burns to lose sight of him behind the desk. "You know, of course, that I was on the committee that recommended Dr. Elmore for the position of dean?"

Aha! Burns thought. "I think I remember that committee," he said. He remembered more, too, now that he had been reminded. He remembered that Elliott, shortly after Elmore's appointment, had been made the supervisor of Vardeman Hall (Hartley Gorman VII), the larger of the two men's dormitories, which meant that in addition to his salary as chairman of speech and drama, Elliott would also receive free room and board for himself and his wife. At the same time, Elliott's wife had been named assistant supervisor of the dorm, at an undisclosed salary. No one knew how much Elliott had managed to sock away thanks to his situation, but his penuriousness was legendary. He and his wife were known to take home doggie bags from nearly every meal.

"Yes," Burns said. "I remember that committee quite well."

Elliott sat back up. "The committee's membership was, of course, known to everyone. What you may not know is that I was the chairman. I was the one who really pushed for Elmore. I was the one who counted the ballots."

"Why are you telling me all this?" Burns asked.

"Well," Elliott said, "I understand that you're cooperating with the police in their inquiries."

"I'm not cooperating with anyone," Burns said. "I was just answering some questions."

"Yes, of course, but you did find Dean Elmore's body, didn't you?"

50

The rumor mill was working as efficiently as ever, Burns thought. Before long, he'd be promoted to special assistant to Boss Napier and maybe be made a member of the FBI. "I found Dean Elmore's body, simply by accident, and that's all there is to it," he said. "I have nothing at all to do with any investigation being conducted by the police."

"Nevertheless," Elliott said, "I'd like for you to know this. In case anyone asks. Everything done by the selection committee on which I served was on the up-and-up. Strictly by the book. I know that there will be talk about that now—not that there hasn't been in the past." He smiled a twisted little smile. "I know what people say about Dean Elmore."

"If anyone asks, then I'll tell them," Burns said, still wondering what all this could be about.

"Fine," Elliott said. "Now the other thing. Do you . . . ah, I mean do the police have any suspects as yet?"

"I have no idea," Burns said. "Really, Don, I don't. My involvement in this is just an accident, as I said. No one from the police is confiding in me. I imagine a lot of other people will be questioned before this is all over."

"I see," Elliott said, in a way that seemed to indicate that he really *did* see, and that what he saw was the fact that Burns was playing it cagey with him. "I see," he said again. Then he got out of his chair and extended his hand to Burns, who rose and shook it. "Thank you for your time. I'd appreciate it if you said nothing of our little chat."

"I won't," Burns said.

Elliott opened the door and left. Burns sat back down and tried to figure out what had happened, but he was unsuccessful. He got up and strolled around to Clem's office.

Clem looked up from a stack of freshman themes. Constant grading was a fact of life for composition teachers.

"So," Burns said, "have you heard the news?"

"It takes news a long time to get to the third floor," she said, "but I've heard. How was the Gestapo?"

"Not bad. Not as bad as you might think, anyway."

51

"And have they corralled the killer?"

"Not yet," Burns said.

"Maybe it was the pregnant woman," Clem said.

Burns laughed. He knew the story to which she was referring. It had happened earlier in the fall. Burns was a member of the Appeals Committee, chaired by Elmore, which heard appeals from those ticketed by the campus police or disciplined by the dean of students. It was rare for anyone to win an appeal. Even the pregnant woman had been unsuccessful.

"She would have been angry enough to do it at one time," Burns said. "Surely she isn't still upset."

"I don't know," Clem said. "I would be."

The pregnant woman had been looking for a parking spot near the Library (Hartley Gorman III) one night during a pouring rainstorm. She was returning some books for a professor in another building, or she wouldn't have been there in the first place. It was nearly closing time, and there were a number of places available right beside the library. The woman parked in the nearest one, returned the books, and came back to her car, only to find a ticket stuck under the wiper blade. She had parked in a faculty place.

Her appeal to the committee was based on the fact that there had been many places available, that she had taken the nearest one, that she had been inside for less than three minutes, that no one else had been inconvenienced, and that she was, after all, eight months pregnant and hadn't wanted to spend a lot of time looking for a more distant student parking place.

Elmore had sent her out of the room. "Obviously," he said, "she's guilty. She did, no doubt about it, park in a faculty place, a clearly marked one at that. Many faculty members have complained to me about student cars in faculty spots. I see no basis for the appeal."

Everyone on the committee agreed, except for Burns, who was overruled.

52

There had been one other appeal since then, this one from a curvy eighteen-year-old coed with honey blonde hair, brown doe eyes, and a low-cut blouse that gave a glimpse of major-league mammaries. She was guilty of putting her parking sticker on the front window rather than the rear window, a crime that the campus police complained bitterly about since they had to get out of their cars to check the sticker. Her excuse was that she didn't know where to put the sticker.

Burns spoke up. "Aren't the directions on the instruction sheet given to the students when they pay for their stickers?"

"I don't know," the girl said in a soft, hesitant voice. "I didn't get an instruction sheet." She batted her long eyelashes as she spoke.

Burns felt compelled to point out that the sticker was stapled to the instruction sheet.

"Oh," the girl said breathily, "then I must have forgotten to read it."

"That can easily happen," Elmore said.

Burns couldn't believe it. "That's your only reason for appeal? That you forgot to read the instructions?"

"Uh, yes, I guess so. I just didn't know," the girl said.

"Of course not," Elmore said. "Dr. Burns, there's no need to taunt the woman. Anyone can make a mistake." He looked at the student with what he probably thought was a mixture of fatherly forgiveness and sternness. "I don't believe there's any need to send this little lady out of the room. I believe she's learned her lesson. Shall we vote?"

They voted, and Burns cast his first guilty vote of the year. He was the only one so to vote, however, and his faith in justice had been severely shaken.

"Maybe it *was* the pregnant woman," Burns told Clem. "If she ever found out about that little blonde, she'd be pretty steamed."

"No jury in the world would convict her," Clem said. "In fact, it's hard to think of a jury that would convict anyone

53

that did Elmore in."

"It won't be easy to find an impartial jury," Burns said. "I do feel sorry for his son, though."

Clem squared off the stack of papers on her desk. "I suppose so," she said. "But have you ever had Wayne in class?"

"No, thank goodness. I've been spared that."

"Well, I haven't, and neither has Miss Darling," Clem said. "I suspect that it's just like certain classes in the 1950s were when spies from the John Birch Society sat in to take notes."

"How do you mean that?" Burns asked.

"I mean that I'm sure Wayne ran to his father with every little tidbit that he could. I mean he was a nasty little spy."

"Gee, Clem, if you didn't like the kid, just say so. You don't have to mince words with me," Burns said.

Clem laughed. "All right, I didn't like him. And he was a wimp. But to tell the truth, I'd put him right up there on the list of suspects if I were investigating this murder."

"Why tell me?"

"Well, you were closeted in with the police, weren't you? That's what everyone says."

"Good grief. Before long, people will be expecting me to wear a deerstalker and smoke a pipe. All I did was answer a few questions."

"Just the same, I know what I'd do," Clem said.

Burns's curiosity got the best of him. "All right, all right. Tell me why. You know I can't stand it."

"He treats that boy just like he treats us," Clem said. "That's reason enough."

"As you tell your freshmen, 'be specific.' "

"Oh, very well. This happened at the beginning of school, during the registration period. You know that our station is on the second floor of the Library?"

"I've worked there for years and years, every semester," Burns said.

"Well, I was going downstairs to get a soda from the machine. I took the back stairs to avoid all those students coming up the

54

front. Wayne was bringing up a box of course plans for some-one on our floor. His father was with him. I don't know exactly what happened, but maybe in trying to avoid me Wayne stumbled. He dropped the box, and course plans flew all over the place. His father called him, I believe, an 'incompetent bozo' and a 'lout.' I was quite embarrassed. I helped pick up the plans, but I wanted simply to disappear. And yet the boy appeared to be devoted to him. Why, I'll never know."

Burns didn't know either, but he said, "Sometimes people respond to that kind of thing. Look at the devotion Vince Lombardi's players had for him."

Clem looked at him blankly.

Realizing that Clem wasn't a football fan, Burns switched comparisons. "Look at Hitler. He was obviously crazy and brutal, but he had quite a following. And then there's Captain Ahab," he said, switching again, this time to literature. "He treated his crew miserably, but they followed him and believed in him."

"I suppose so," Clem said, "but it's sad in a way."

"Of course it is. But even children who are physically abused, and I mean severely physically abused, cry when they're taken away from the parents who abuse them."

"That's even sadder," Clem said.

Trying to lighten the mood, Burns said, "Besides, if everyone who was called a 'bozo' by Elmore got in line to kill him, the one at the end would starve to death before he got his chance."

Clem smiled. "That's certainly true."

"Didn't he even call the chairman of our board a bozo in one of our monthly faculty meetings?"

"I believe what he said was, 'Just because a man is chairman of the board doesn't mean he can't be a bozo,' " Clem said.

"Maybe the chairman killed him," Burns said.

"Too many suspects," Clem said. "Sounds like a good title for a book."

"Probably already been used," Burns said.

55

7

MISS DARLING CALLED out to Burns as he tried to slip past her office, so he stepped in. Miss Darling wore a high-necked white blouse and looked a bit like a doll would look if dolls had old faces instead of young ones.

"I just heard about poor Dean Elmore," Miss Darling said. She was probably the only person who would refer to him that way.

Burns moved her purse out of the chair by her desk and sat down. He often wondered what women carried in their purses to make them so difficult to move. "Yes," he said. "It's very sad."

"There's no need to be sarcastic, Dr. Burns," Miss Darling said. "I know that Dr. Elmore has had his differences with most of the faculty, but his death *is* sad. Remember what Donne says: 'No man is an island.' Not even a department chairman."

Miss Darling was undoubtedly right, but somehow Burns did not feel diminished by Elmore's death. If anything, he felt as if his horizons had been considerably expanded. So he didn't say anything.

"Still," Miss Darling continued, "I did truly believe that his plan for the school was an evil plan. I'm glad that it will not be put into effect."

Burns agreed.

"I hope that your discovery of the . . . ah . . . corpse did not discompose you," Miss Darling said.

Burns was surprised to find that he was not in the least discomposed, nor had he been. One might have thought that

57

he found dead bodies every day of the week, so little effect had the experience had on him. He wondered if he was particularly cold-blooded or merely normal. "No," he said. "I feel fine. Maybe I can only be affected by literature. The real thing doesn't seem to bother me."

"Pish," Miss Darling said. She was the only person Burns had ever known who actually said "pish." "I'm sure that you feel as deeply for your fellow man as anyone does."

"I suppose so," Burns said, and maybe it was true. He didn't exactly regard Elmore as his fellow man, however.

They discussed Elmore's death a few minutes longer, but without any speculation as to who would take his place. Burns was sure that Miss Darling would fall right in line, no matter who it was. In fact, by the time a successor was appointed, Miss Darling might have forgotten the whole thing.

Back in his office, Burns decided to stay at school for the rest of the afternoon. Often he went home on Tuesdays, although he had to drive back in the evening for his once-a-week class in American fiction, which met at six o'clock. Today, the drive home didn't seem worth the trouble, even though it took only five minutes. Tonight's novel was *As I Lay Dying*, and Burns thought it might be a good idea to spend the afternoon looking over a few articles and skimming through the primary text again.

He spent two hours in study, then looked in his middle drawer for his lists. There were several that he had tossed in, including one on which he was trying to list the ten great American novels. This was a list that he'd tried more than once and never gotten very far on. One day he wanted *Huckleberry Finn* in the top spot, and the next he wanted *Moby Dick*. Then the day after that, he wanted *The Sound and the Fury*. At that point he'd usually decide that the list was too conventional anyway and toss it aside. He'd never gotten past the number five in any attempt he'd made.

The fact that he'd never finished didn't bother him, however. The purpose of the lists was relaxation and

58

stimulation, not definitive enumeration. The lists were just something he did for fun, the way some people worked crossword puzzles or played bridge. Crossword puzzles generally bored him, and he could never remember how to respond if his bridge partner should happen to bid one no-trump. So he made his lists.

Today, however, he couldn't get interested. It had gotten late, most of the faculty had gone home by three or four o'clock, and it was now after five. The building was most likely completely deserted, and Burns sat listening to the sounds it made.

Occasionally the wind would rattle the windowpanes, which were quite loose in their frames. The putty that held them was shrunken and dried, and chunks of it had long ago fallen out. The rafters would creak, and every now and then the old radiators would pop and clang as the steam from the school's decrepit boiler surged and receded.

This was the time of day that Burns liked the building best, when it was almost as if it belonged to him. He thought for a second about the pigeon shit above his head, and then he wondered if it were symbolic. He looked up at the ceiling tiles that Mal Tomlin assured him were all that lay between Carl Burns the man and Carl Burns the guano statue. There was an ominous dark stain on one of the tiles, as if the roof had leaked and the water had run through some vile substance before soaking into the tile. If he stared at the stain long enough, it assumed the shape of a pigeon.

He'd been reading Faulkner too long, he thought. He picked up *As I Lay Dying* again and began to thumb through it. "My mother is a fish," he read.

The class went well, no students being moved to ask about the death of Dean Elmore. Most of them even appeared to have read the book, and a few even had intelligent questions to ask. The only problem was that at about seven-thirty the heat began to fail. The builders of Main had never really

59

heard of the benefits of insulation, so by eight o'clock most of the class had on their coats and sweaters. Burns dismissed them before it got so cold that they were distracted from the discussion.

After class, Burns locked his office and visited The Rat. The Rat was in the men's room, located on the second floor. Main having only one restroom per floor, the first and third floors had gotten women's rooms.

The Rat had first appeared in late summer, shortly after one of Rose's periodic campaigns to wipe out the rodent population. It was easy to keep up with these campaigns because when they began green and white boxes of poison would appear in both likely and unlikely places. There were usually several in the history lounge, and there were always plenty in the restrooms.

The Rat, Burns speculated, was a victim of one or more of those boxes. At first only his tail appeared, discovered by Earl Fox as he opened the door to one of the two toilet stalls in the men's room, which had not been noticeably improved since it was first used by Hartley Gorman himself. There was a good inch of space between the floor and the back wall, and the toilet crouched crazily at a slightly tilted angle. There was a wide, thin board attached somehow to the back wall, which was of the original stone. All this had been painted white, a color that did little to take away the stall's resemblance to a medieval torture chamber. Burns always half expected Torquemada to leap out at him when he opened the door.

The Rat had never leaped at anyone. It was too dead for leaping, but its tail was enough to scare Fox into the screaming meemies. He had exploded out the men's room door yelling incoherently and disturbing classes not only in Main but probably in every other building on campus. Burns had been in the history lounge at the time, and he had run out to see what had happened.

Fox was standing in the hall, his knees together like

September Morn, one hand in his mouth and the other pointing at the men's room door. Burns went in and opened the stall door. The Rat's tail was hanging straight down from behind the board attached to the back wall. The tail looked tough and leathery, and it was banded like a snake.

No one ever figured out how a rat, which must have been of considerable size, since Mal Tomlin measured its tail precisely at eight-and-a-half inches in length, could have gotten between the board and the wall to do its dying, but it was indisputably there.

And there it remained. Rose adamantly refused to touch it. "I ain't 'bout to touch no dead rat's tail," she informed Fox and Burns when they told her about it. "I ain't gone touch it even with gloves on, and that's all they is to it. Let 'em fire me if they want to."

Burns and Fox didn't blame her, and being firm believers in the chain of command they didn't go over her head to her supervisor. They just left the rat there as a conversation piece, and it came to be known as The Rat.

As summer wore into fall, The Rat began to dry out and slip a little lower down the wall. Burns figured that maybe in a couple of years it would finally slip completely out and fall to the floor. At the present time, however, only the tail, part of its rump, and its two back paws could be seen. It gave a man something to reflect on as he faced the commode for relief. There had been no urinals in Hartley Gorman's day, and there were none now.

Having paid his respects to The Rat, Burns went downstairs to his car. Tonight, sitting on the frigid vinyl seats was like sitting on a glacier. But the car started immediately, and the heater would be working after a few blocks.

Burns liked to stop for a pizza after his night class, so he drove to the Pizza Delight, a local, nonfranchise establishment that was generous with its toppings and not too heavy on the sauce. It wasn't too heavy on decoration, either, and the interior was mostly rough wood. There were a

61

number of plain tables with formica tops and no cloths, surrounded by metal chairs with hard wooden seats. Burns ordered a pizza with everything, except anchovies, which he
hated, and looked around for a place to sit.

Someone motioned to him from the dimly lighted rear
tables, and he walked back. It was Mal Tomlin and his wife.
Burns joined them.

Mal was smoking a cigarette, as usual. "I was just telling
Joynell about you finding the dear dead dean," he said as
Burns sat down.

"It must have been horrible," Joynell Tomlin said. She was
a direct contrast to the compact muscularity of her husband,
being somewhat tall and chubby. Her face was round and
soft, like the Pillsbury doughboy's, and her hands were fat
and pink. She didn't powder her hands. She was also given
to blonde wigs that were nearly as spectacular as those worn
on stage by Dolly Parton, though the wigs were where any
resemblance ended, except possibly in the mind of Joynell.

"It wasn't so bad," Burns said. "I guess I was too surprised
to be shocked."

Joynell uttered a disconcerting titter. "Oh, no," she said.
"I didn't mean that you'd be *shocked*. I bet *no*body is shocked. That man was bound to get killed, just by being who he
was. I just mean it must have been a horrible sight."

"Let's not talk about it while we're eating," Mal said. He
and Joynell had already gotten their order, a large pepperoni
pizza, most of which had probably been consumed by Joynell.

"Oh, we've just *got* to talk about it," Joynell said. "Tell me,
Carl, did you ever hear about what Elmore tried to do to
Mal?"

"Uh, I'm not sure," Burns said. Elmore had done so many
things to so many people that it was hard to keep up with
what he'd done to whom. Or tried to do.

"It's ancient history," Mal said. "Let's just forget it. '*De
mortuis nil—*' "

"None of that Latin stuff, honey," Joynell said, reaching

62

for the last slice of pizza lying on the round metal plate. She turned to Burns. "He was going to strip Mal of his chairmanship and put Clark Woods in."

Burns was amazed. "You're kidding," he said, laughing. "Not Clark Woods, the Young Philosopher. Why didn't you tell me about this?"

Joynell took a huge bite of pizza and chewed meditatively, leaving Mal to answer. "It wasn't anything, really. I don't think anything would ever have come of it even if they hadn't found out about Woods."

What "they," meaning Elmore, had found out was that Woods had been seducing coeds with some regularity. He was a good-looking young man, around thirty, who looked like a younger version of Frank Gifford and who in fact had been quite a collegiate football player. He also looked exactly like a "real" college professor should look, as opposed to someone like, say, Earl Fox. Woods wore tweedy jackets with leather patches on the sleeves, and fisherman's knit sweaters, and Clark's desert boots. He was always quoting Dewey or Piaget, gaining his nickname from his frequent reference to their works. After one girl's husband had complained about him to the administration and produced certain incriminating evidence (rumor had it that the evidence was his wife's tearful, tape-recorded confession), Woods had departed the campus for groves of academe unknown.

"I can't believe it," Burns said. "The Young Philosopher."

"Believe it, kiddo," Joynell said, having finished off the triangular wedge of pizza in about three king-size chomps. "I thought Mal was going to have a stroke when he told me about it."

"It was a long time ago," Mal said, "right after Elmore took over as dean. I'd almost forgotten about it."

"I bet," his wife said, wiping her mouth with a paper napkin.

"What were you supposed to do? Quit?" Burns asked.

Mal mashed his cigarette in the ashtray. "Nothing like

63

that," he said. "I'd just become a regular faculty member. No reduction in salary, even. Of course, Woods would have been my boss."

Joynell had reached under her chair for her purse, opened it, and found a tube of lipstick, which she was applying generously to her pouty mouth. "You can imagine how much Mal would like *that*," she said, never missing a stroke.

Burns leaned back in his chair. "But why? I mean, what did Woods have that you don't have?" He paused. "I mean besides looks, sex appeal, and a full head of hair." Tomlin was sensitive about his thinning hair, and Burns regretted having said anything as soon as the words had left his mouth. Tomlin didn't seem to notice, however.

"I don't know. Certainly my qualifications are as good as his. We both went to the same school, though admittedly he was there ten years after I was. I never did quite figure it out, and then I didn't have to. Woods wasn't around to worry about."

Joynell snapped her purse shut. "Don't let him pull your leg, kiddo. He knows all right, and so do you. It's those cigarettes." She gave Mal a hard look. "I've told him time and again to quit smoking those things."

Burns thought she was probably right, though being an English teacher he looked for the symbolism in what she said rather than the literal meaning. Mal smoked as much to defy the administration as he did for his own enjoyment of nicotine. He simply wasn't a team player. Woods had been a team player, and he only seduced girls in the privacy of his own home. Had it not been for the guilty conscience of one young woman, Woods would probably be Mal's boss right now.

"It's funny, isn't it, honey?" Joynell said to her husband. "I remember how you came home that day and said you'd like to kill that Elmore. 'Bash his head right in,' you said. And now he's gone. How *did* he die, Carl?"

"Ah, someone bashed his head in," Burns said.

"Now isn't that a coincidence!" Joynell squealed.

Mal looked uncomfortable, as if his pizza hadn't quite agreed with his digestive system. He squirmed in his chair.

Burns looked down and then to the side. He was embarrassed, though he didn't quite know why.

"Why, just look at you two," Joynell said. "You'd think you were both guilty. You look like two little boys that got caught with their hands in the icing bowl."

Mal gave a shaky laugh. "Listen, Carl," he said, "I wouldn't want you to think—"

"I don't think anything," Burns said. "It's just a coincidence. That's all it is." He tried a laugh himself. It sounded pretty sincere to him.

"Number fifty-nine, your order is ready," a voice announced on the speaker.

"That's mine," Burns said.

"We've got to go now," Mal said. "See you tomorrow."

"Yeah, see you tomorrow. Good night, Joynell." Burns got up and went for his pizza. Somehow, he wasn't hungry anymore.

8

BUNNI CAME IN between the nine and ten o'clock classes the next morning to tell Burns that there would be a special faculty meeting that afternoon at four o'clock. It didn't require too much imagination to figure out what the subject of the meeting would be.

There was also something else on Bunni's mind. "Dr. Burns, you don't think that what we were doing—I mean the picketing and all—you don't think that had anything to do with what happened to Dean Elmore, do you?"

"I'm sure it didn't, Bunni. How did the pep rally go, by the way?"

Bunni's face became animated. "It was great. You should've been there, Dr. Burns. Just about everybody in the dorms was there, and Coach Thomas made a speech about school spirit, and George talked about how much being on the team meant, and . . . well, it was really good."

"I knew it would be," Burns said. "I know that even Elmore would have been convinced that he was making the wrong move as soon as he heard about it. You did have someone from the school paper there taking pictures, I hope?"

"Oh, sure," Bunni said. "They were going to run them on the front page, and on the sports page, too."

Considering that the paper usually had only four pages, that was pretty good coverage, Burns thought. "Well, I wouldn't worry about Dean Elmore," he said. "The police might want to talk to you if they find out about the picketing, or they might not. They may already have some suspects."

"Do you really think so?" Bunni asked eagerly, as if she fully expected Burns to know.

"I'm not in the confidence of the police, Bunni. I'm sure they'll let the public know whenever they find anything out."

"I guess so," Bunni said. She turned to leave. "I'll be at my desk if you need anything."

"Thanks, Bunni," Burns said. She went out of the office, back to the other side of the third floor. Her desk was in a sort of outer office that fronted the offices of three other members of the English Department, the three who were rarely seen and who were known to the rest of the faculty as Larry, Darryl, and Darryl. They came on campus, taught their classes, and went home. They never complained about their schedules, they never questioned administrative caprice, and in fact they seldom did anything more than what was required of them by their jobs. All three were men in their late thirties, all three had been at HGC for more than ten years, and all three did a respectable job in the classroom. If they were asked to come in early for a meeting, they did. If they were asked to teach extra classes, they did. No one knew them very well, but Burns had no reason to complain of their work. They left him alone, and he left them alone. They were probably the three least likely to be affected, in any way, by Elmore's death.

As Burns sat thinking about his faculty, the phone rang. It was Boss Napier, who wanted to have a little chat. Burns told him to come at eleven o'clock.

Napier had on the same leather jacket, but a different pair of boots. He was panting and winded by his climb up the stairway to the third floor. "I swear to God, Bends, I don't see how you do those stairs every day."

"That's Burns. And I sometimes do them five or six times a day. You get used to it."

"I don't think I would. Can I sit down, or what?"

By getting to his office before Napier arrived, Burns had

68

given himself time to assume what he imagined the business psychologists would refer to as the "power position." He was seated comfortably behind the wide expanse of his executive desk in the best chair in the office. He graciously asked Napier to be seated, but the police chief had to sit in the "conference chair" placed by the desk for student-teacher conferences. It didn't seem to bother Napier a bit.

"There are a few things from our little talk yesterday that we need to hash over again," Napier said after he was seated.

Burns waited. He wasn't going to be any help, not that it would make any difference. As soon as the word got around that Napier had been to see him, and it would get around fast, he would be rumored to be either arrested or cooperating with the police. He wasn't sure he cared for either idea.

"You didn't see anybody enter or leave the building, right?" Napier asked finally.

"Right," Burns said.

"You're sure."

"I'm sure."

"I thought you would be. You know, the more I think about it, the more I like *you* for the kill. You were there, you didn't like the guy . . ."

How did he know that, Burns wondered. Obviously he'd been talking to other members of the faculty.

". . . and you certainly had the opportunity to use the blunt instrument on him."

"What blunt instrument?" Burns asked.

Napier crossed his legs, flicking his western-cut pants to straighten the crease. "We don't know that for sure yet," he said. "We do know that Fenimore hadn't been dead more than a few minutes when you found him."

"Elmore," Burns said absently. He was wondering just what Napier was trying to tell him. "You still haven't found that paper-clip holder?"

"Not yet," Napier said. "You know, we don't get many homicides in Pecan City. We made a few mistakes in this one."

"Such as?"

"We should've sealed off the whole building, not just that one office. Oh, we still searched, but there were so many people coming and going that anyone could've carried that thing out."

Burns thought of something. "Whoever killed Elmore, and it certainly wasn't me, could have been in the building all the time. I didn't make any extra noise going up to Elmore's office, but in that empty building I must have sounded like a herd of elephants. Someone could have been hiding in the office next door or in the rest room down the hall. Then he could have mingled with the people coming back from assembly."

"Yeah," Napier said, "but you just thought of that. I thought of it last night. I wish I'd thought of it a lot sooner. But like I say, we don't get many homicides here. I'm just learning."

There wasn't much Burns could say to that.

"What do you know about this Coach Thomas?" Napier asked, changing the subject.

Burns was amazed that he'd gotten the name right. "Not much. He's a pretty good coach, but he doesn't have much material. If he could get some good athletes, I think—"

"Cut the crap, Stearns. I don't give a damn about his football team. I want to know about that scuffle he had with Elmore in the lunch room. You were there and saw the whole thing."

Next thing you know, he'll even get *my* name right, Burns thought, though he wasn't counting on it. "Whoever told you that I was there can tell you as much as I can," he said. "There wasn't any scuffle, however."

"Whoever told me that you were there said there was a scuffle."

"Well, there wasn't," Burns said. "Elmore might have thought that Coach Thomas was about to rough him up, but it didn't happen. Elmore just got scared and fell out of his

70

chair."

"You've got to admit that Thomas really had it in for Elmore, though."

"I don't have to admit anything," Burns said. "Coach Thomas was upset and maybe a little excited about Elmore's saying that he planned to drop the athletic program, but that wasn't Elmore's decision to make. A lot was already being done to prevent it, and Thomas knew it. He didn't 'have it in' for anyone."

"So you say," Napier said. "What about this Belinda Edgely woman?"

"Dorinda," Burns said patiently. "We went over that yesterday."

"Not enough," Napier said. "I hear that last year at that Kiss a Pig contest, she got really upset with Elmore, maybe even said something to him."

Burns tried to recall what he'd heard. He hadn't attended the actual consummation of the contest, but someone had told him what had happened. "I think she said something like, 'There's more than one pig here today.'"

"And he said, 'You and that one over there makes two,'" Napier said.

"That's what I heard," Burns said. "It's only a rumor."

"You think it was a cover-up?"

"Cover-up?"

"For hanky-panky," Napier said.

"No," Burns said.

"There's that snout, though," Napier said.

"Yes," Burns said. "There's that snout."

Down in the history lounge, Burns and Fox didn't discuss Napier. Burns was trying to recall the details of another run-in that Thomas and Elmore had had.

Fox was smoking Players Lights today, and the ashtray was a Dr. Pepper can. "Twenty-five in a pack," he said. "You can't beat a deal like that, except maybe for those generic cigarettes at Kroger. But I really hate those tacky yellow packages." He brushed some ash off the knit shirt he was wearing, a brown, white, and blue number with a fishlike pattern woven into it. "I remember the time you're thinking about. It really didn't involve Thomas so much as one of the assistant coaches. What was his name—Handy? Camby?"

"Hamby," Burns said. He wasn't smoking. He'd burned the roof of his mouth on the pizza the night before, and it tasted as if the Chinese army had marched through, using his tongue as a door mat. A cigarette wouldn't help. "Claude Hamby. Adonis himself. I remember the whole thing, now."

Claude Hamby had been an assistant coach the year Elmore had become dean. Hamby was a bodybuilder whose idol was Arnold Schwartzenegger. Though Hamby's own development didn't really rival Arnold's, it wasn't bad, especially for a place like Pecan City, where most of the residents looked and dressed like bit players in *Red River*. Hamby was fond of displaying what he had, and he loved to take off his shirt at football workouts and expose his delts and pecs. He always wore short, tight white shorts.

Though Hamby could have had his pick of the eligible women in Pecan City (of which there were very, very few, in Burns's opinion), he seldom showed any interest, a fact that had caused more than a little talk in certain circles.

That talk was nothing as compared to what came later, however, after Hamby's final fling. It happened on a warm Indian summer afternoon one Sunday in late October. A newly married couple, the husband a devout ministerial student, his wife the daughter of missionaries, went for a picnic on a piece of land outside town. The land was owned by Coach Thomas, and it was widely known among the students that Thomas never went there and that he didn't mind if they enjoyed a picnic beside the little stock tank that nestled behind a small dam out of sight of the road.

There was a little wood that ran right up to one bank of the tank, almost, and it was at that spot that the young man

72

and his wife settled down to enjoy the afternoon. They were saying grace over their meal when they heard a rustling in the trees, and they had just stood up to investigate when Hamby stepped out between two oaks. He was stark naked.

The young woman swooned. Her husband turned red. Hamby fled back into the trees.

By the time the ministerial student reached town, the story had come to include two boys, also naked, standing beside Hamby. The student went straight to Elmore.

Hamby denied that there was anyone with him. He also made it clear that he had Thomas's permission to stroll around his property, naked if he pleased. It seemed that Hamby had a bit of the nudist in his blood, and a nude stroll was something that he required every now and again for his general well-being and peace of mind.

Thomas had confirmed the story. The student recanted the part of *his* story about the two nude boys. Elmore was livid and demanded that Hamby be fired anyway. Thomas supported Hamby, who had nevertheless quit at the end of the semester. The brouhaha had been too much for him.

"That bozo better consider himself lucky if he lands another coaching job closer to this state than Outer Mongolia," Elmore was reported to have said. In truth, Hamby got a job at a major school in the Southwest Conference, a fact that galled Elmore sorely.

"Yeah," Fox said, "but all that was three years ago. You don't think Elmore still held that against Thomas, do you? Or that Thomas would kill Elmore because of it?" He considered the idea for a minute. "Besides, didn't President Rogers defend Hamby, sort of halfheartedly?"

"Yeah," Burns said, "and don't think *that* didn't cause a lot of talk. Took a year to die down. Anyway, I'd say that the answer to your first question is a great big "Yes." *Of course* I think Elmore still held Hamby against Thomas."

He thought a second, then grinned. "I don't mean that the way it sounds. Anyway, Elmore could hold a grudge longer

73

than any man alive. In fact, I wouldn't be surprised if that was the very reason the football program was going to be put down the tubes. It took Elmore three years, but he finally got enough ammunition to take to the board. Damnit, I'm almost sure of it."

He leaned forward and took a Players out of the pack. He'd decided to have a smoke after all.

Fox lit up too, just about the time Dorinda Edgely pushed open the door. Fox's cigarette, which had been on the way to his mouth, hit the floor.

Burns recalled one time when they had been smoking in Fox's office and someone had knocked on the door. Fox had put his cigarette in the ashtray—a real glass one, not a Dr. Pepper can—put the ashtray in his desk drawer, and shoved the drawer closed. A student had come in, asked a few questions about an exam, and left. When Fox opened his desk drawer, smoke billowed into the room and Burns had nearly strangled. The smoke alarm near the ceiling went off, and they had to go to Rose's closet for a ladder so that they could remove the battery.

Dorinda didn't deign to look at the burning cigarette, but she did glance all around the room. Her face was drawn, and there were black circles beneath her eyes. Her stretch pants were still stretched to the limit.

"Can we help you, Dorinda?" Burns asked.

Dorinda's eyes darted into the nooks and crannies of the room, of which there were plenty. Rose didn't like to clean in there because the room hadn't been remodeled with the rest of the building; the baseboards were dingy, and the walls were streaked. Dust had gathered in the dimly lit corners.

"I'm looking for something," Dorinda said.

"We sort of gathered that," Burns said. When Dorinda's eyes focused in on Burns, Fox took the opportunity to ease his chair closer to the burning cigarette and put his foot in front of it.

"I thought I might have left it in here," Dorinda went on.

74

Burns had a good idea of what it was that Dorinda was looking for, but he didn't want to say so. "Nothing in here but me and Dr. Fox."

"I can see that," Dorinda said. Then, more to herself than to them, she said, "I must have lost it *some*where."

Burns got up and dragged the only other chair in the room, a warped metal folding chair that looked hardly able to bear his weight, up to the table. He sat down and indicated the chair he had vacated by waving the tip of his cigarette at it. "Have a seat, Dorinda," he said.

Dorinda looked for a moment as if she would run, but then she shrugged and sat down.

Fox sighed and stepped on his still-glowing cigarette.

"Dorinda," Burns said, "I think I know what you're looking for. And I think I've seen it recently."

Dorinda, who had leaned slightly forward in her chair, sat up straight. "No!" she exclaimed. "It wasn't mine! It couldn't have been mine!"

"I think it could have been," Burns said. "Or else you wouldn't be looking so hard for it now. Retracing your steps, so to speak."

"I never went near that office," Dorinda said. She seemed to shrink a little in the chair. "I told that policeman that, but I don't think he believed me. It's true, though." She paused. "He kept calling me 'Miz Sedgefield.' "

"Don't let that bother you," Burns said. "He has a problem with names. And I think he must have heard that you had a problem with Elmore last year."

The reference to Elmore perked Dorinda up. "I called him a pig," she said. "And he was. Besides, I've heard him called a lot worse."

"I've called him worse myself," Fox said. "What's this all about?"

"The snout," Burns said.

"Oh," Fox said.

"But it couldn't be mine," Dorinda said again.

75

"Then where *is* yours?" Burns asked.

"That's what the policeman wanted to know." Dorinda looked at Burns with suspicion. "Are you working for him?"

"I'm just an English teacher," Burns said. "Despite what you might have heard."

"Well, I don't know where my snout is," Dorinda said. "I don't see what difference that makes, though, since I never went near that office."

"Can you prove that?" Burns asked.

"You sound just like that policeman. No. I can't *prove* it, but doesn't he have to prove I went there?"

"If I sound like Boss Napier, it's only because I'm trying to apply a little logic to this," Burns said. "If Napier can prove that snout under Elmore's head is the same one you were wearing, you might be in considerable trouble." He dropped his cigarette in the Dr. Pepper can, wondering idly what kind of can would be there tomorrow. The cigarette had long since gone out.

"I just don't understand," Dorinda said. "I must have lost my snout somewhere. I thought maybe it was in here. I thought that if I could just find it . . ."

"Well, it's sure not in here," Fox said. "Where else did you go that day? When did you miss it?"

"That's just it. I didn't miss it. I must have laid it down somewhere and then not thought of it again."

"I guess you'll have to keep on looking," Burns said. "But I'm afraid you won't find it. Where did you go after you left here?"

"I'm not sure," Dorinda said. "I think I went to the ladies' room."

76

9

THEY WAITED UNTIL the crowd of students had cleared the halls after the eleven o'clock classes, and then they waited a minute or two longer. Burns and Fox had never been in the ladies' room before, and they wanted to be sure that they didn't shock anyone.

They needn't have worried. Dorinda marched up to the dark green door and pounded on it with her fist. "Anyone in there?" she yelled. No one answered, so they all three went in.

This room was much nicer than the men's room downstairs. There was no rat, for one thing. For another, the stone walls had been covered with Sheetrock, which had then been textured and painted. There was a large mirror over the sinks, and there was a couch under the window. The only jarring note was the sign taped to the mirror:

PLeAse!
Do not!!
SpiLL PowdeR !!!
in thE Sink !!
MAid Rose

Dorinda looked in the stalls, and Burns looked beside the sinks and beside the trash can. No snout.

"Look," Fox said. "If you'd left the snout in here, Rose

would have thrown it away anyway. There's no way it would still be in here."

"I'm almost sure this must be where I left it," Dorinda said, her eyes scanning the room. There was a fluorescent light, in addition to the frosted windowpane, so there was no dark corner for the snout to be hidden in. "Maybe someone picked it up."

"You aren't even sure you left it here," Burns said. "Just keep on looking. And just hope no one saw you going into the library that day."

Dorinda just looked at him and then walked out, leaving Fox and Burns alone in the ladies' room. "I think we better get out of here before someone comes in," Fox said. "Although it would probably start the best rumor in some time."

They got out.

Faculty meetings were always held in the chapel of the Bible Building (Hartley Gorman IX). Burns, Fox, and Tomlin walked in together at four o'clock exactly and sat on the thin red cushion in one of the back pews. One of the music teachers was playing a slow and mournful version of "Amazing Grace" on the old Wurlitzer electric organ. President Rogers was seated behind and to the left of the podium, wearing a black suit and a somber expression.

Most of the rest of the faculty had arrived by the time Burns was seated, and he hardly had time to reach for a songbook before Rogers was on his feet. "Let everyone stand," the president said, "and join in singing hymn number two hundred thirty-eight, "What a Friend We Have in Jesus." He raised his arms. Everyone stood, and the organist surged into "What a Friend."

Burns looked around as everyone sang. Hardly anyone bothered to look at the hymnal, the song being such a familiar one. There wasn't a wet eye in the house.

Then the song was over. "Let us all remain standing," Rogers said, "while Dr. Swan leads us in prayer."

78

All the heads automatically went down, and Abner Swan stepped out of his pew and walked to the front. It was not a long walk, since Abner habitually sat on the front row, the better to impress the administrators.

"Oh, God, our heavenly Father," Abner began, and then went on to bless the school, its founders, its faculty, its students, its administration, and its board, the "great nation we all live in," and "especially the family—of which we feel that we are all a part, Dear Lord—of the late Dean Elmore, a man who did his part to make Hartley Gorman College the fine institution of higher learning it is today." Abner went on to ask for guidance, strength and direction, as well as wisdom and compassion. By the time he finally said "Amen," Burns was beginning to wonder if he thought he was preaching an Easter sermon.

Swan's "Amen" was echoed around the chapel by a number of others, and everyone sat down. President Rogers remained standing behind the podium and looked out at them. Then he began speaking. He had a good evangelical style, Burns thought. Nothing flashy, nothing to cause Jimmy Swaggart to lose any sleep over, but effective nonetheless. He knew when to shout, and he knew when to whisper. He knew when to get a catch in his voice, and he knew when to be straightforward and manly.

The gist of his message was that although the school had suffered a great tragedy and a lot of unwarranted publicity— even the television stations in Dallas had carried the story— Hartley Gorman College would recover and go forward. That although Elmore had been a great leader (and here Burns had looked around to see if there was anyone else biting his lip and trying not to snicker), God would send another leader to take his place. That although Elmore's forward-looking vision would be sorely missed, perhaps some of his innovative plans could be carried out. (Burns sincerely hoped that they wouldn't be.)

Rogers then announced that Elmore's funeral would be

79

held on Friday afternoon at 2:00 p.m. at "the church." No one had to ask which church that meant, since whenever anyone at HGC referred to "the church," he meant the First Baptist Church across the street from Main. In conclusion, Rogers said that he knew that Elmore's death could in no way be related to HGC and that the person or persons responsible were no doubt outsiders who had sneaked into the administrative offices in the hope of robbing them. Surprised in their activities by the valiant dean, they had killed him and escaped.

Burns was genuinely surprised at this last bit of information, and he looked around to see if anyone else was buying it. Few seemed to be paying much attention, though some were looking up speculatively, as if here was an angle they hadn't thought of. As far as Burns was concerned, there was good reason they hadn't thought of it—it was hogwash. He had been on the scene, and he knew that Elmore wasn't the victim of a botched robbery attempt. Rogers was obviously trying to keep everyone from thinking what some of them already were: that there was a murderer among them.

Rogers asked for a moment of silent prayer, and then they all sang "Oh, God, Our Help in Ages Past."

As the books were slipped back into the racks and the feet began to shuffle, Fox turned to Burns. "Did you buy all that?"

"I believe we got some publicity," Burns said. "I just hope we don't get any more."

Burns was sitting at home that night rereading Ross Macdonald's *The Chill* when a thought occurred to him. The sinks in the ladies' room, there being two of them, sat on a long green cabinet. There had been doors on that cabinet, but no one had opened those doors when he, Dorinda, and Fox had searched the room. It wasn't impossible that Rose, if she had actually found the snout on the sink corner, had put it inside the cabinet for safekeeping. It seemed highly doubtful that she had, but it was something

80

that should be checked. For that matter, they should have asked Rose herself if she had found it. It wasn't always easy to find Rose, however, and Burns had often wondered when she wrote and posted her notes. He had seen many notes over the years, but he had never seen Rose taping one to the wall.

Then there was Rose. Burns found himself wondering if she had ever had any difficulty with Elmore. What if she had found the snout, carried it over to Elmore's office, and conked him with the paper-clip holder? She certainly seemed at times to possess the power to make herself invisible. It was all highly unlikely, but . . .

Burns returned to his book, but he found that he couldn't concentrate. He was afraid he'd been bitten by the detection bug. Before long, everyone would be right about him. He'd be cooperating with Boss Napier.

He'd rather be Lew Archer, though, or Philip Marlowe.

He got up and walked around his room, his finger marking his place in *The Chill*. The whole thing bothered him more than he had allowed himself to admit. He was restless, and he couldn't stop thinking about it.

He looked at the clock. Nearly eleven. Too late to do anything, really, but after all he did have a key to Main. He could go down and look in that cabinet. That would take his mind off things and calm him down. No one would ever even have to know.

He put on a blue knit sweater, got in his car and drove toward the school. He would have to be careful, since the night watchman, referred to by most of the student body as "Dirty Harry," was said to have an itchy trigger finger. "Harry" was a retired policeman—long retired. Guesses at his age ranged from seventy-five to eighty and up. No one knew for sure. All they knew was that he was a short, dried-up man who looked far too small to carry the gun he wore on his belt, a heavy .44 magnum that he'd been known to pull on anyone who crossed his path after eight o'clock at night.

81

And they also knew that after about ten o'clock he retired to the boiler room and slept in a straight-backed wooden chair that he tipped against the wall. So Burns figured that he would be pretty safe if he entered Main.

The weather had been cold and overcast for several days, and the nights were the same. An occasional drop of rain hit the Plymouth's windshield as Burns drove toward the school, but nothing big enough or frequent enough to require the wipers.

Burns parked on the street outside the building. There were no other cars in sight. The parking lot near the Administration Building was deserted. He got out of the car and started up the walk. There was no way to sneak in the building—not that he intended to sneak—since it was lit on three sides by huge floodlights. However, Burns was not worried about anyone's seeing him and alerting Dirty Harry; there was almost never anyone on the streets of Pecan City after ten o'clock, and tonight was no exception.

Burns got out his key and entered. The old wooden doors were hardly a deterrent to burglars, since a good push was all that was really required to open them, even without a key. He locked the doors behind him, though, so that if the watchman did check he would find them secure.

With the heat off for the night, Main was cold and dreary. Burns didn't mind. He liked the musty, dusty smell of the old building, and the floodlights outside gave plenty of illumination by way of all the windows. Burns walked along the hall and to the stairs.

The stairs had been carpeted at one time, and they still were, but only in a manner of speaking. The carpet had been subjected to so many years of HGC students' footsteps that it was worn completely away in places, which made it dangerous if one wasn't careful. A shoe toe or heel could easily be caught and cause a serious fall. But Burns went up the steps confidently, even in the semidarkness. He knew them too well to worry about falling, though one teacher no longer with the school had fallen and broken her coccyx in broad daylight. She had been forced to carry a rubber doughnut with her to sit on for months afterward. ⁻

It was darker on the third floor, but Burns had no trouble reaching the ladies' room. He pushed open the door and flipped the light switch, then stepped inside. The door closed quietly behind him. He didn't think that Dirty Harry would see the light through the single frosted window, and besides, Harry was probably sound asleep in his chair in the boiler room by now.

Stepping to the sinks, Burns pulled open the cabinet doors. There was nothing inside except four rolls of industrial-strength toilet paper (some people preferred to call it "bathroom tissue," but Burns felt that "tissue" was far too gentle a name for this stuff, which he was positive could be used to sand automobile bodies in preparation for painting), two red-white-and-blue canisters of Ajax cleanser, and a stiff-bristled brush with a long wooden handle.

Just to make sure that there was nothing else, Burns moved the rolls of toilet paper aside, but there was nothing behind them. The snout was definitely not there. Burns closed the cabinet. Well, he thought, he'd just have to ask Rose in the morning.

He flipped off the light and reached for the door handle. That was when he heard the noise.

Main, being old, made a lot of noises. The rafters creaked and the windows rattled. Sometimes you might even hear a rat scuttle across a ceiling tile. And sometimes still a pigeon would get into the attic and beat around.

This noise was different. It was a solid thump, as if someone had bumped into something. And it seemed to come from the attic.

Burns stood still, his hand on the doorknob, waiting for his eyes to get accustomed to the darkness. His first thought was that Dirty Harry had indeed seen the light and come to investigate. But the noise was definitely not in the right spot to have been made by someone coming up the stairs.

Opening the door slowly, Burns stepped out into the hall. The light was faint, but had anyone been there he would have seen him.

There was another noise, different this time, but clearly from the attic. Something strange was going on, and Burns was going to find out what it was. He felt very protective toward the old building, and now he suspected a student prank, though that would be in worse taste than most HGC students would indulge in, considering the recent death of the unlamented dean.

In the past, there had been such pranks, though not during Burns's tenure at the school. He had heard the stories, one of which concerned several erstwhile scholars who had led a mule up the stairs of Main and stationed it in the spacious cupola over the north classroom, the one in which Burns taught most of his classes. There wasn't enough noise for a mule this time, but *some*thing was going on.

Burns walked to the head of the stairs. To his right was the door to his classroom. To his left was the hallway that led to his office by way of Clem's and Miss Darling's offices. But just before the hallway there was a door. Facing the head of the stairs, he also faced that door, which was always kept locked. Behind the door was a large storeroom, and at the back of the storeroom was the stairway that led to the attic. Burns had seen the stairway, but he had never put a foot on it.

Burns tried the door. It was unlocked. He pushed it open.

There was no light in the storeroom, but there was a window. Burns could make out the stacks and stacks of cardboard boxes that contained the collected English themes of generations of HGC students. In theory, the papers were kept in storage for two years, then disposed of. In fact, some of the boxes probably held themes that were ten or more years old.

Elmore had recently made one of his rare trips to the third floor—in fact, his only trip, if Burns remembered correctly—

84

and discovered the trove of paper. Unfortunately, Elmore had been in the company of the local fire marshal, and the storeroom had been declared a fire hazard. Elmore had supposedly hired his son and another student to clear out all the old boxes, leaving only those collected within the two-year limit, but so far nothing had been done.

Burns made his way through the stacks of boxes, some of which came up to his shoulders, until he came to the stairway. Nothing in this room had ever been remodeled. The floor was bare planking, and the walls were yellowing plaster. The stairs were crudely fashioned from four-by-sixes. Obviously, many an HGC student had been in the room at one time or another; the plaster was covered with names and dates scrawled or neatly printed over the years. Burns couldn't read any of the names or dates in the dimness, but he had read them before. The earliest date he had seen was 1913, along with a name written in pencil. He'd often wondered what had happened to the student who wrote it, and if he ever remembered the moments he'd spent there by the stairs putting his name on the wall.

There was another noise from above. Burns put his foot on the first step and started up.

There was another door at the top of the stairs. This door, too, was always kept locked, but it was not locked now. It was standing slightly ajar. Beyond it was deep darkness.

Burns went through the door. He stood quietly, hoping that his eyes would adjust to the absence of light. He could hear the noise more clearly now. There was definitely someone in the attic, someone who was walking around very carefully.

There was some light in the attic after all, coming in through small cracks and also through some of the original stained-glass windows that had once extended from the third floor on up into the attic. Most of these had been boarded over, however.

To Burns's right was some sort of partition or wall, and

there seemed to be some kind of walkway under his feet. He put his hand on the wall and started walking. He was being as quiet as possible, since he had decided that whoever was in the attic shouldn't be there. He would try to see who it was without being seen.

There was a strong ammonia odor, and Burns thought of what Mal Tomlin had said about the pigeons. Just then, the wall ran out and Burns's hand groped into darkness. He felt forward with his right foot. The walkway had ended, too.

Burns stood on the walkway, waiting and listening. He could hear someone moving around, and now he could hear something else, as if the person were muttering to himself. Then there was a sloshing noise, followed by the sound of liquid splashing. Burns smelled gasoline.

The very thought of what a fire could do to Main made Burns turn to his right, toward the area over his office, stepping carefully from rafter to rafter, feeling for each one with his foot. At about the point where Clem's office ceiling was, he was stopped by a massive black object, darker than the surrounding darkness. He put out his hand and touched it. It was metal. He moved his hand along it.

He had heard stories that the original steeple that had first topped Main was located in the attic, but he had never thought much about them. Apparently, they were true.

He began working his way along the steeple, which tapered slowly downward. His feet on the rafters were moving through dust and piles of something he was sure was pigeon shit, but it was dry and he tried to ignore it. He also tried not to think about how much of it was piled in the spaces between the rafters.

As he got to the end of the steeple, virtually kneeling to keep his hand on it, he saw a tiny beam of light, probably from a penlight, coming from the area above his office. The area was an alcove, however, and the wall shielded whoever was in there.

Burns straightened up, ready to step to the next rafter,

when he heard a loud yell, followed by a curse. Burns was so startled that he almost fell, but he managed to retain his balance by wildly waving his arms. He heard a rampant scuttling, and squeals, and then a crash as something heavy, like a gas can, flew through the air, hit a rafter, and bounced off.

"Goddam rats! Brrrrrrrgh!" someone yelled.

Burns started forward cautiously.

Then he saw another light. The person had struck a lighter!

"Burn, you sonofabitch," the someone said in a calmer voice. "Burn."

10

CARL BURNS WAS not a man who often thought of himself as having a heroic nature; in fact, he had probably *never* thought of himself as having a heroic nature. But he couldn't just stand by and do nothing when faced with the imminent possibility of the destruction of a building he loved. Besides, he didn't see any way either he or whoever was holding the lighter could get out of the attic alive. Main was, if anything, a genuine firetrap.

So he screamed, "Stop!" as loud as he could and tried to run forward across the rafters.

Whether from surprise or intent, Burns didn't know, whoever was in the attic dropped the lighter. It flickered between the rafters for a moment, and then the fire caught.

Burns fell on it, and a great many things happened at once. Only later did he manage to sort them out in his mind.

Before he was aware of any heat or burning, the flooring of the attic gave way with a crash. Somehow he managed to get both hands on a rafter and hang on. Dust, dirt, pigeon shit, flooring, and who knew what else crashed down to hit the acoustical tiles that had been installed during the remodeling of the building years before. There was a hollow thudding as the debris hit the tiles, but the tiles remained in place.

Because the fire had barely begun before Burns fell on it, it had been extinguished, though when he glanced down he thought he saw a spark or two. Nothing to worry about. He hung, swaying, on the rafter, his nose full of the smell of dust and gasoline. His shirt front was filthy against his chest, and his hands were beginning to hurt where the wood of the rafter bit into them.

Someone was crashing around in the attic, heading away from Burns's position. It wasn't long before he heard the drumming of feet on the stairs, and then all the sounds died away. In a surprisingly short time, it had grown very quiet.

Burns didn't know exactly what to do with himself, but he knew that he couldn't hang on much longer. He also knew that he was no athlete, and he doubted that he could hoist himself back into the attic. He made an attempt to chin himself up. No luck. He tried to swing his legs, thinking that he might be able to hook a foot over the rafter and then haul the rest of his body after it. That didn't work either.

There was, of course, the other alternative, which in a few minutes would be a necessity instead of a choice. He looked down at the tiles beneath his feet. The tiles had stopped the trash that fell, but they wouldn't stop him.

He didn't think about it for very long. He took a deep breath and let go.

He tried to hold his legs and body straight, but he was hardly conscious of falling before his feet struck the tile. There was little or no resistance as it split under his weight. Then he tried to relax, bending at the knees. Still, when he hit the third floor, he hit it hard.

His legs took the shock and then he was rolling. He didn't roll far, because he had struck the floor in the narrow hall right in front of his office. Dirt, boards, pigeon shit, and pieces of acoustical tile showered down on him.

Burns lay there for a few minutes on the worn carpet, trying to take stock and see if anything was broken, bleeding, or beyond repair. He decided that there wasn't, but when he finally stood up and tried to put his weight on his ankle, he experienced a sharp pain.

He brushed his hand through his hair, trying not to look at what fell out, slapped at his pants, and opened his office.

He hobbled around behind his desk, sat in his chair, and called the police.

Boss Napier was not pleased. His western shirt was wrinkled, and his hair stood up here and there in little spikes. Burns suspected that he had been fast asleep. They sat in Burns's office and listened to the noises from above as Napier's men searched the attic.

"So you just decided to come down and look for that snout on the spur of the moment," Napier was saying. "Just like that. At night. All alone."

Burns was wishing he had one of Fox's cigarettes. "That's right," he said. "To tell the truth, I didn't really think I'd run across a crazed arsonist."

"We have only your word that there was anyone else in this building," Napier said, kneading his left fist with his right hand. Burns wondered again if the stories he'd heard about Napier might have a basis in fact.

"You found that lighter," Burns reminded him. The lighter had been in the pile of debris in the hall. "Maybe it'll have prints on it. And you could check the doorknobs. Of course, I touched those, too."

"Of course," Napier said, kneading away.

"But the lighter . . ."

"We'll check it, don't worry. But even if there are prints on it, they may not do us any good."

"Why not?" Burns asked.

"Because for the prints to do any good, they've got to match up with something. If the prints aren't on file, they won't do us any good. How many people who work here've been fingerprinted, would you say? Not counting those that've been in the army?"

Burns thought about it. "Probably not any."

"Probably," Napier said. "So then what do we do?"

Burns thought about it, then admitted that he didn't know.

"Me neither," Napier said. "We'll have to come up with a suspect, and a pretty good one at that. We can't just go around forcing everybody to submit to fingerprinting."

Burns didn't say anything, but he wasn't sure that the mass fingerprinting wouldn't succeed. If Elmore had thought of it, he probably would have done it himself, and gotten away with it. After all, Elmore was the one who came up with the idea of the "Statement of Firm Belief," and he'd gotten away with *that* one.

The "Statement" crisis was one that Burns had found unbelievable despite all his prior experience at Hartley Gorman College. It had all started when a perky blonde coed had gone home and told her daddy, who just happened to be the minister of a fairly influential church, that she thought some of the HGC faculty members were closet commies who didn't believe that every single word of the Holy Bible was literally true. The King James Version, that is, the one with the words of Jesus in red. One of the dastardly liberals, unidentified by the daughter, had dared to imply that perhaps the dreaded theory of evolution was more than just a theory. And, she said, it was rumored around the campus that someone (again, no name) might possibly have once voted for George McGovern in a long-ago presidential race.

It was all too much for the girl's sainted father, who descended on HGC clad in the full armor of God and waving his King James translation over his head like a battle flag. He demanded nothing less than a full house-cleaning, a purging of those anti-Christian, anti-American elements that had infiltrated the HGC faculty, said purging to take place immediately, if not sooner.

Elmore, who knew a good thing when he saw it, agreed wholeheartedly. He had called a faculty meeting, at which Abner Swan had prayed endlessly, the father had fulminated interminably, and Elmore (with Rogers standing smiling by) had emerged as the voice of reason. Or so he wanted it to appear. He had a modest proposal.

His proposal was that each faculty member would sign a Statement of Firm Belief, of which he just happened to have a hundred or so copies handy, in which said faculty member swore his belief in the literal truth of the Holy Bible, his hatred for the evils of secular humanism, and his devout belief in, as Burns remembered it, any number of other things, including baptism by total immersion.

Burns, and quite a few others, had been completely taken aback. Burns sat stunned, thinking about the Great Loyalty Oath Crusade in *Catch-22*, and its purpose of making everyone agree with the leaders and scaring the hell out of those who didn't.

It had been Earl Fox, of all people, who spoke out, Fox, who wouldn't ever smoke a cigarette in front of another teacher, much less an administrator. Burns was amazed.

"The way I see this thing," Fox said, standing in the pew and resting his hands on the back of the pew in front of him, "the way I see it, we'd practically have to be Baptists to sign this statement."

The coed's father had risen to his full height. "And what, may I ask, is wrong with that?" he roared, in the rolling tones of a prophet of old.

"Probably nothing, sir," Fox said. "Except that some members of this faculty are members of other churches."

You could have knocked the father over with a pew cushion. The look of shock on his face was one that Burns would long remember. It was as if the man had been told that the faculty was composed of atheists and sodomites.

Elmore had stepped forward, put his hand on the man's arm, and led him to a seat, where he sat with head bowed, praying, no doubt, to be delivered from this pit of heathenism.

Elmore returned to the pulpit. "Dr. Fox," he said, "I see no reason why any thinking person, any *right*-thinking person, cannot sign the document I have proposed. It contains nothing to contradict the doctrine of any established church.

I believe that any person who wishes to remain in the employ of Hartley Gorman College will sign the document, and sign it now. Otherwise, he will leave this room freed of any obligation to this school."

"But our contracts," Fox said.

"Nothing but paper," Elmore said. "Nothing but paper."

Fox sat down, and pens began scrawling on paper.

Nothing but paper, Burns told himself, rationalizing like mad, and certainly less valid than my contract.

Everyone in the room, whether by the same rationalizing process that Burns used or through genuine conviction, signed the paper. Including Fox. But Elmore had disliked Fox from that time forward. Many people thought that Fox's days at HGC were numbered.

Burns didn't say anything to Napier about the "Statement of Firm Belief," but he knew that any faculty that would fall in line for something like that certainly wouldn't balk at a little thing like fingerprints.

Napier's men came down out of the attic and were standing outside Burns's office door. One of them was holding a gasoline can gingerly by the spout. "This is all we could find up there that looked like it might help us out," he said. His shoes and pants were dusty and matted with spider webs. "There's a lot of messing around been goin' on up there, but there's no way to tell who did it." He gave Burns a hard look.

"All right," Napier said. He gestured at the can. "Take it down to the station and have it printed. We'll see what we can come up with."

The two men turned and walked down the hall. Napier stood up. "I'm still not sure what your part in all this is, Buns, but I'm going to try to believe that you've been telling me the truth so far. I just wish things wouldn't happen with you around all the time."

"That's Burns. And I really don't like the things that happen to me any more than you do."

Napier turned to leave, then turned back. "Just one thing.

What's the connection? Did the same person who killed El- more do this? And if he did, what's the motive? You're a col- lege professor. Come up an answer for that one."

"To tell the truth," Burns said, "I haven't even thought about it."

"Think about it, then," Napier said, and went out down the hall.

Actually, Burns *had* been thinking about it. He just hadn't wanted to share his thoughts with Napier because they weren't fully coherent yet. He had tried to think why anyone would want to burn Main, and he could think of only one reason. Money. He had no idea what the building was in- sured for, but he thought he might try to find out. Just who would try to collect, he didn't know. It was a scheme that would have suited Elmore's character perfectly, but Elmore was dead. Rogers? Could this be just another money-making scheme, one planned by Rogers and Elmore, along the lines of the degree mill? Burns could imagine the English, history, and education departments split up and housed in various temporary quarters around the campus while Elmore and Rogers decided how to spend thousands of dollars in in- surance money.

It was then that Burns realized that Napier had made another mistake, and so had Burns. It had been so late that Burns had decided not to disturb Rogers with a call, and Napier had agreed that it would be better to call him early the next morning. After all, no real damage was done.

But what if Rogers had been the man in the attic?

Burns didn't like to think about it. Still, it was possible. Burns got out of his chair and limped to the door. He decided to worry about it in the morning.

By the time he arrived at school for his eight o'clock class in composition, Burns had thought things through. Whoever it was that had tried to burn the building, it wasn't Rogers. The man in the attic had been angry and thoughtless. Stupid,

95

in fact. He should have realized that he was as likely to go up in smoke himself as to burn the building. Rogers would have found a better way. Certainly he wouldn't have been splashing gasoline around. He would have been calm and deliberate, not emotional like the man in the attic.

So who was it? And why had he done it? And was there any connection with Elmore's death? Despite his earlier resolve, Burns felt himself being drawn into things. He hadn't ordered his deerstalker yet, but it wouldn't be long.

Burns climbed the stairs to the third floor. Rose, who came to work at seven o'clock, had already cleaned up the mess from the hall in front of his office. President Rogers had also been on the premises. There was a note taped to the office door requesting that Burns report to Rogers's office as soon as he got out of class. He pulled the note off the door and went in. His ankle still hurt, and he knew he would have to teach his class sitting down, something that he preferred not to do.

He still had ten minutes until the bell, so he scratched out a list of "Ten Characteristics of a Good Essay." It would give him something to talk about in class, and it would take his mind off all the extracurricular events that were bothering him. After class, he would go to see Rogers.

Rogers's office was right across the hall from Elmore's, and Burns noticed that there was even a door into the president's inner office, which would have looked directly into Elmore's had the door been opened. The door, however, was permanently locked, and Burns had to enter a large room that housed Rogers's secretary and her own huge desk, a couch, a coffee table, two chairs, and several potted plants. The couch and chairs were covered in a gold material that more or less matched the carpet. The plants looked as if they would have preferred to be outside, and the magazines on top of the coffee table were so old that Burns was sure one of them was an issue of *Collier's*.

96

Rogers's secretary stood up behind her desk when Burns entered. She had grown old on the job, and Rogers was the third president for whom she had worked at HGC. Her mostly gray hair was pulled back into a severe bun, and she wore glasses that swept up at each end of the plastic frames. Burns hadn't seen anyone wearing glasses like that since the 1950s.

"Good morning, Dr. Burns," she said, in a surprisingly firm voice. "Dr. Rogers will see you right now. Just go on in."

She motioned toward the door of the inner office, and Burns thought of the two titles she had just used. His own had been earned by five years of graduate work at the state university, with another year of work on the dissertation. Rogers had gotten his at a graduation ceremony at which he hadn't really graduated. The degree had been conferred on him for his many services to education and to his church. It was a common practice. Burns had even heard of trade-offs, sort of "you give our guy a degree and we'll give your guy one" deals that made two men instant owners of the title of "Doctor." After a few years, most people had forgotten where the title came from, and the title itself was all that really mattered.

The situation didn't really bother Burns. He understood that in the academic world, illusion and reality worked just about like they did anywhere else. Rogers had been a long-time minister, with a leaning toward administrative skills. A powerful friend of his had been on the school's board. When the presidency of the school came up for grabs, Rogers grabbed. And he held on.

Burns went through the door. Rogers was seated behind a desk so big that it could have been used for table tennis. Burns was sure that it must have been brought into the office in sections and assembled there. On the wall of the office opposite the immense desk were bookshelves, most of them filled with books like *The Life and Teachings of Jesus* and *How to Win Friends and Influence People*. In the middle of the wall behind the desk was the locked door, and hanging on either side

97

of it were numerous photographs of Rogers shaking hands with, or standing by, famous people. Here was Rogers with Billy Graham. There he was with former Governor Briscoe. And there he was with Roy Rogers and Dale Evans. The wall on Burns's left had similar photographs, all framed in gold. The wall on the right was mostly windows, tastefully draped.

Rogers sat in a large, overstuffed red leather chair. There was a similar chair in front of the desk, though it was not on a swivel base as Rogers's was.

Rogers did not stand. Burns thought that he was sensitive about his height, or lack of it. "Have a seat, Dr. Burns," Rogers said, motioning to the chair in front of the desk.

Burns sat. The chair was firm and comfortable, but when he looked at Rogers across the expanse of the desk, Rogers seemed miles away.

"Dr. Burns, it seems that someone is out to destroy and discredit Hartley Gorman College," Rogers said. His voice, certainly not as mellow and fruity as Abner Swan's, was nevertheless as effective in a private conversation as in a public meeting. "The question is, *who*?" He looked at Burns as if he expected an answer.

"I really have no idea," Burns said.

"But you seem to be on the scene when things happen," Rogers said. "Not that I'm implying anything," he added, when Burns didn't speak.

"I'm a victim of circumstance," Burns said. "I don't know what's going on, and that's a fact."

"The police seem to think otherwise," Rogers said, leaning over the desk and steepling his fingers.

Burns wondered what Napier had told Rogers when he called. "They're wrong, then," he said. "I had an appointment with Dean Elmore, and I just happened to find his body. I just happened to come to school last night and interrupt an arsonist. I know that sounds feeble, but it's the truth."

Rogers changed tacks. "I can't imagine why anyone would wish to take the life of Dean Elmore," he said.

Burns didn't respond. Rogers wasn't *that* dumb.

"Of course, I suppose he did have his faults," Rogers finally said, "but which of us doesn't?"

Maybe he was that dumb. Burns decided to find out. "I hate to speak ill of the dead, but let's face it: Elmore had more faults than most people around here. Most of us have never figured out why he was ever chosen to be dean in the first place."

Rogers looked shocked. He folded his hands, and they disappeared behind the desk. "Why, he was chosen by a committee," he said. "I'm sure the committee thought he was the best man for the job. There could be no other reason."

"Of course," Burns said.

"Well, then," Rogers said. "I just wanted you to know that I'll be doing all I can to help the police in their investigations. I hope that all of this is cleared up soon. And I'd like to thank you for what you did last night. Were it not for you, Main would be a heap of ashes and stone at this moment." He stood up and held out his hand. Burns had to strain himself to reach it, but he managed. They shook, and the meeting was over.

Burns left, with one thought on his mind. He was going to call Don Elliott and have a little chat.

11

ELLIOTT WAS PUFFING from his climb up the stairs, a feat that had rendered him temporarily speechless. Burns waved him to a chair, and they waited until Elliott was breathing more or less normally before beginning their conversation.

"I know why you called," Elliott said, his baritone restored.

"You do?" Burns asked, surprised. He wasn't even sure himself.

"Of course," Elliott said, and Burns was once more amazed that such a powerful voice could come from such an apparently frail body. There were more distinctive voices at HGC than seemed right for such a small institution. "Everyone's talking about me, and the police have asked you to pump me for information. I knew it would happen."

Burns recalled their earlier conversation. He was beginning to suspect that Elliott was a little paranoid. Or maybe he was feeling guilty about something.

"Look," Burns said, "no one's talking about you, and the police can do their own pumping. They're much better at that sort of thing than I am. But I did want to talk to you about that committee you served on."

Elliott gave a theatrical sigh. "I knew it," he said. "I knew it would come to this."

"Come to what?" Burns was already feeling exasperated, and they had just begun talking. "I haven't even asked you anything yet."

"Ha," Elliott said, enunciating clearly and mournfully. "Ha-ha."

"Don," Burns said, trying to keep his voice level, "I'm just another faculty member. We're colleagues. That's all this is, just a meeting between two colleagues. I'm not some undercover secret agent."

Elliott seemed to shrink even more. If he'd been blue, the casting director for "The Smurfs" would have spirited him away. "So you say. So you say. But everyone knows about how someone tried to burn this building last night and you stopped him. Falling through the flooring and all." He glanced over his shoulder at the hall, though there was no way he could see the hole in the ceiling. "You were up here with the police half the night, from what I hear, searching the building for clues."

Ah, the HGC rumor mill, Burns thought. If Elmore could have turned out degrees at half the speed the school could generate rumors, he would have died happy.

"All right," Burns said. "Have it your way. But remember, I'm telling you the truth. This is just information *I* want. I may give it to the police later, but right now I'm asking for me. To satisfy my own curiosity. As far as I know, this is something the police haven't even thought of." And if I know Napier, he won't think of it at all, Burns almost said. He restrained himself, however.

"I understand," Elliott said. It was clear that he didn't believe a word that Burns had said.

"Good. So what's the real truth about how Elmore got to be dean? You counted the votes, you said."

"It's your friends that have been talking about me, isn't it?" Elliott asked. "Fox and Tomlin. They're the ones. Aren't they?"

"Don, just answer me. Man to man. No one else is involved. I promise."

Elliott did not look reassured, but he finally answered. "Yes, I did count the votes. But that's not where it all started." He wiped his hand across his forehead. "Elmore was actually a pretty good candidate. He was in-house, and

102

therefore he was familiar with the school and the faculty. He knew all about our programs and our operations. In fact, he'd really done his homework. We had some prepared questions, and he answered all of them very satisfactorily."

"But Don," Burns said, "everyone hated him."

"Of course, there was that," Elliott said. "A personality problem, we called it. But look at it from the committee's point of view. The other candidates were from out of town. They didn't know our situation here. And how were we to know they wouldn't turn out to be as obnoxious as Elmore?"

"So Elmore was clearly the best candidate, and he was chosen on that basis?"

"It could have been that way," Elliott said.

"Don't give me 'could have been,' Don," Burns said. "Did he get the votes or not?"

"I don't know," Elliott said. His head was down, and he didn't meet Burns's eyes. His voice was still controlled, but it was very low.

"You don't know?" Burns was taken aback. "You don't know? But you said that you counted the votes."

"I was *supposed* to," Elliott said, still without looking up.

Burns thought about it for minute. "I see," he said, and he thought he did. "The fix was in. It didn't matter who everyone voted for. Elmore was going to win."

"That's true," Elliott said. "But no one on the committee ever made any protest. It's possible that they *did* vote for Elmore."

"Possible," Burns said, "but it didn't matter. Okay. Why did you do it?"

Elliott looked up, but he didn't say anything.

"I always wondered about you and your wife getting that dormitory job," Burns said. "Elmore couldn't have arranged that, not so soon after getting the deanship. It had to be Rogers." He looked sharply at Elliott. "It was Rogers, wasn't it?"

"Yes," Elliott said. His voice was was so subdued that

103

Burns almost didn't hear him, quite unlike Elliott's normal voice. "He came to me during the interview process and said that he really hoped that Elmore would get the job."

"That's all?"

"He . . . he said that he'd been thinking about that dormitory job. I'd asked him about the vacancy earlier. I'd invested some money unwisely—nearly all my savings—and I needed to recoup. He hinted that if Elmore became dean, I'd get the dorm. That's all, just a hint. But I made sure that Elmore was the man."

Elliott finally looked up at Burns. "And no one on the committee ever complained. Probably most of them did vote for Elmore."

"None of them ever takes credit for it," Burns said. "Rogers didn't give you any idea *why* he wanted Elmore?"

"No," Elliott said. "He never said."

Blackmail at HGC? Burns wondered. It just didn't seem possible that Elmore could have anything on President Rogers. After Elliott left, Burns, like Miniver Cheevy, thought and thought and thought about it.

But he couldn't come up with anything.

A little later, Fox turned up at Burns's office door. "Want to go see someone kiss a pig?"

Burns had been thinking so much about the snout that he'd forgotten about the actual contest. "Why not?" he said. "You think it's still on?"

Fox was sure. "You don't think a little thing like the death of one of the participants is going to stop an event of this magnitude, I hope. The show must go on, and besides, it's all for the scholarship fund."

"You think Dorinda will be there?"

"That's part of the fun," Fox said. "And we can see if she's found her snout."

Burns got up and went with him. They stopped on the first floor for Mal Tomlin, and the three of them walked to the student dining hall. The weather had improved considerably; the sun was shining, and the sky was a clear blue. The temperature was near sixty degrees.

Mal Tomlin was smoking a cigarette, and the ashes blew back on Fox's jacket, a moth-eaten red-and-black number with a high school letter on it. Fox brushed the ashes off and admonished Tomlin to be more careful.

"I didn't know you played football in high school, Earl," Tomlin said.

"I didn't," Fox told him.

"Then where did you get the jacket?" Tomlin asked.

"There was this big garage sale over on Lindale Street—" Fox began.

"Never mind," Tomlin said. "I should have known."

They entered the men's dormitory, bypassed the faculty dining room, and went straight on into the student dining area. There was a girl sitting at a table, and in front of her was a cigar box. Burns, Fox, and Tomlin each paid her two dollars, which she put in the box. Then they got green plastic trays from a high stack and entered the line.

The room had a low ceiling and a cement floor; consequently it was extremely noisy. Students were sitting at wooden tables and talking, laughing, and even yelling. In the kitchen, pots, pans, and utensils were being washed, dried, and banged into drawers or thrown into bins. Now and then an empty plastic glass would hit the floor and bounce hollowly.

The three instructors got their plastic plates and their napkin-wrapped utensils. Then they were served. The food was about what they had expected: mashed potatoes, stringy green beans, carrots, and a batter-fried meat patty of indeterminate origin.

After being served, they went to a drink dispenser. Burns got water, the others got soft drinks. Then they located an empty table and sat down. As they picked at their food, they looked around for other faculty members. Coach Thomas was there, sitting morosely at a table with Fran Stafford and Joe Reasoner. Abner Swan was at a table with several other members of the Bible Department. Burns didn't recall their names, but he recognized their white shoes. And Dorinda Edgely was there, sitting at a table with several students.

It was too noisy in the hall for real conversation, so the three men continued to make a pretense at eating while waiting for the big moment. It wasn't long in coming.

The tone of the noise changed around them, and Burns looked up. Struggling through one of the side entrances was none other than George ("The Ghost") Kaspar. In his arms was a squirming, kicking, squealing member of the pork brigade. Not a full-grown hog, of course, but a sizeable pig.

Tables were shoved aside by cheering and laughing students as George made his way toward the center of the room. Bunni was trailing behind him.

When they arrived approximately where they wanted to be, George set the pig on the floor. There was a rope around its neck, and George held one end. The pig strained against the rope, emitting an eager squeal, but George held tight.

Bunni waved her hands for quiet. Someone banged a fork against a plastic glass, which did no good at all. The chattering and laughter continued. Finally, Bunni put two fingers in her mouth and gave a piercing whistle. It grew quiet immediately.

Burns was amazed. He had never realized that Bunni had talent. He would have given a lot to be able to whistle like that, but he had never been able to master the art. Maybe Bunni would teach him.

George began making a brief speech. "I'd like to thank you all, on behalf of the student government, for making our contest such a big success again this year," he said. "Your contributions have added over three hundred dollars to our scholarship fund." There was a round of halfhearted applause. "The big winner this year, with over a hundred and fifty dollars turned in, is"—George paused for effect—"Miss

106

Dorinda Edgely!"

Burns looked over at Dorinda, who didn't seem nearly as happy as she should have at her victory. Leave it to Elmore to spoil even the smallest moment of triumph, even if he had to do it from beyond the grave.

Looking past Dorinda, Burns spotted someone he hadn't noticed earlier. Wayne Elmore was leaning against the far wall, looking as prissy as ever, and even more contemptuous. He was quite a good-looking boy, actually, but the perpetual sneer on his lips detracted a great deal from his appearance. Burns wondered what his home life must have been like. With Elmore for a father, it wouldn't have been good. You never knew, though, Burns thought. Some of the most faithful dogs were the ones most mistreated by their masters. Burns then wondered why Wayne was there at all; it seemed a bit disrespectful to his father's memory for the son to be attending a frivolous contest on the day before the funeral. Maybe Wayne had hoped to defend his father's title, or to get a chance to kiss the pig if his father had happened to win.

Dorinda was making her way to the center of the room, and Burns turned to watch. She had almost gotten there when the pig got loose.

George later said that he must have momentarily relaxed his grip in the excitement of the moment. Burns, however, would always believe that George let go of the rope deliberately, just to see what would happen.

In any case, the pig was loose, and an excited pig is quicker on his feet than one might think.

The pig made a run straight at Dorinda, who was momentarily paralyzed by the sight. Bunni, faster of wit than Burns would have believed, stamped her foot down on the end of the rope.

Both women went ass over elbows, Bunni because the knot in the end of the rope jerked her off balance, and Dorinda because the pig ran right into her slightly bowed legs.

There was instant chaos. Some people were leaping to the

aid of the fallen women, while others were chasing the pig, some of them giving their ideas of the Arkansas razorback hog call. The hog calling caught on quickly, and cries of "OOOOOOOOOOOOOOEEEEEEEEEE!!! P-I-I-I-G! SOOEY!!" rang all around the room.

The probably deafened pig dashed this way and that, skittering desperately as it tried to gain traction on the hard floor.

The only one who seemed to remain calm in the melee was Wayne Elmore. Burns would have liked to help out, but Fox was laughing so hard that he was weeping, and Burns began laughing as well. The sight of Dorinda landing on her stretch pants had done them in.

Wayne Elmore, on the other hand, acted as if he were accustomed to dealing with crises of this nature every day. He waited calmly by the wall, and when the pig flashed by, he reached down quickly and cleanly, snatching the rope, grasping it firmly, and planting his feet.

The pig was brought up short, the rope choking off its piercing squeal. Its feet shot right out from under it, and it hit the floor with a thud that shook dust from its hide.

Fox, who had almost regained some semblance of calm, began laughing again, so hard that he had to put his head down on the table. Even Mal Tomlin was cracking up by now.

With a look of complete disdain, Wayne took several loops in the rope and began dragging the pig back to where George still waited, his hand on Bunni's arm. Dorinda still sat with legs splayed out on the floor, and she recoiled as Wayne dragged the resisting pig past her.

George took the rope, and Wayne swished away without a word.

It was several minutes before the crowd quieted enough for George to speak again. Even at that, he was interrupted from time to time by choked guffaws from Earl Fox.

"Well, faculty and fellow students," George said, "I hope this won't become a feature of our annual event." There

108

were boos and cheers. The students plainly liked the idea of a repeat performance.

"To continue," George said when things quieted again, "Miss Dorinda Edgely has won the honor of kissing this year's pig." He looked for Dorinda. "Could someone please help Miss Edgely to her feet?"

Several students belatedly dashed to the rescue of the fallen professor and helped her to her feet. She looked anything but eager to kiss the pig, but she gamely started forward. She'd wanted this honor for years, and she wasn't going to pass it up.

George very carefully handed Bunni the rope, then scooped up the pig in his arms. Dorinda gave it a hasty peck on the snout. The students whistled and cheered.

"You know," Fox said, "it reminds me a little bit of *Romeo and Juliet*. Then he began laughing again.

But Burns was thinking about Wayne Elmore.

12

IT WAS WHILE he was watching the ten o'clock news that night that Burns thought of something that made him wonder if he hadn't missed an important point. Worse yet, it appeared that Napier had missed it, too.

The point was, that if someone had tried to burn Main one night and been thwarted, what was to keep him from trying it again the next night? The answer, as far as Burns could see, was that nothing could stop him, unless Dirty Harry were on the ball. And if Harry were on the ball, it would be the first time.

Burns got in his car and headed for the school. It was only when he got there that he thought of calling Napier.

What had appeared so normal and innocent the night before, now appeared sinister and threatening. The flood-lights bathed the old building in an eerie glow, and shadows from the tall pecan trees that surrounded it played over the walls and the vacant, eye-like windows. The vines that grew on the building's sides were dead and leafless, and they looked like the veins in the back of an old man's hand. The shrubs that grew close around the building's sides looked as if they might conceal all sorts of pyromaniacs.

Burns shook off his sense of foreboding. I'm beginning to feel like a character in "The Fall of the House of Usher," he thought as he started up the walk. The walk had once been lined with honeysuckle, and Burns remembered the rich, heavy scent. Elmore had ordered the honeysuckle chopped down the first summer after becoming dean; he felt that the water bill was too high. That Elmore. What a great guy.

As Burns mounted the steps, there was a rustling in the bushes. He started to turn, but there was something cold and hard in his ear.

"Freeze!" someone said.

Burns's first thought was that the arsonist had returned, with a gun this time. Then he thought of Dirty Harry. Only then did he think that Napier might not have been quite as slow on the uptake as Burns himself had been.

"Now then," the voice said, "put your palms against the door."

"It's all right," Burns said, attempting to turn, "I'm . . ."

The gun barrel jabbed into his ear, not gently, and was given a little twist. "Palms against the door! Now!"

Burns did as he was told.

"Legs back . . . good. Now spread 'em."

Feeling like a character on a TV show, Burns spread his legs. The gun barrel left his ear, and a hand patted him up and down, very carefully.

"Look," Burns said, "I'm a professor here. If you'll just look in my right back pocket, there's identification."

A hand lifted out his billfold. Burns began to turn once more, and the gun jabbed him in the backbone.

A flashlight came on, and after a minute someone said, "All right, Dr. Burns, you can turn around now. Maybe you'd like to explain what you're doing down here."

Burns turned and faced a young policeman in uniform, a flashlight tucked under his left arm and Burns's billfold in his left hand. His right hand held the pistol, though it was not pointed directly at Burns any longer.

"I'm sorry," Burns said sincerely. "I just thought that maybe the arsonist might try again. So I came down to check." It sounded lame, even to Burns.

"Sounds to me like you don't have much faith in your local police," the young cop said.

"It's not that," Burns said, lying. "It's just that . . . uh . . ."

"Here's your billfold," the policeman said, handing it over.

112

Burns took it and stuffed it in his back pocket.

The policeman put his gun in its holster and secured it with a leather thong that snapped to the holster. "I know how it is. You guys that don't get much action like to think you can help the cops solve the crimes. Like that old lady on that TV show. What's it called? The one where she's a writer?"

Burns sighed. "Murder, She Wrote," he said.

"That's the one. That old gal always knows what the cops don't know. Well, let me tell you, Dr. Burns, it doesn't work like that in real life. We're the pros. We know what we're doing. Boss Napier told me about you. He says you always turn·up in this case. You could get in trouble like that, you know?"

Burns knew. "I've already had enough trouble," he said.

"Good," the cop said. "Why don't you go on home and leave this stuff to us, huh?"

Burns went on home.

The next morning Burns was sitting in his office reading over an article on Hawthorne in preparation for his ten o'clock class. He was teaching "My Kinsman, Major Molineux" that day. His feet were up on his desk, and he was leaning back, comfortable in his executive chair.

He was thinking about the Freudian implications of Robin's staff when Bunni came in.

Burns put down the book he was holding, but he was too comfortable to take his feet off the desk. Bunni had seen him that way too often to be bothered. "Where'd you learn to whistle like that?" he asked.

Bunni was not her usual high-spirited self. "I didn't learn," she said. "It's just something I can do." She twisted her hands together. "Can I talk to you about something?"

Burns swiveled around, moving his feet to the floor. "Of course."

Bunni looked over her shoulder. "Privately, I mean."

Burns got up, walked around the desk, and closed the

113

door. Bunni was obviously worried about something. "Have a seat," he said, returning to his chair.

Bunni sat down. "I . . . I talked to that policeman yesterday."

"What policeman?" Burns asked, though he had a pretty good idea.

"The one they call Boss," Bunni said.

"He's really not so bad," Burns said. "Don't let him worry you."

"It's not me," Bunni said, with a sob in her voice. Burns was afraid she might cry. He wasn't good with crying. "It's *you!*"

"Me?" Burns hadn't been expecting that. "Why me?"

"Oh, Dr. Burns," Bunni sobbed, "I *had* to tell the truth. I just couldn't do anything else."

"Of course you couldn't," Burns said, wondering what was going on. "I wouldn't expect you to lie. The truth never hurt anyone." The threat of tears had reduced him to platitudes.

"I'm so glad you understand," Bunni said. "I told George that you would, even it if meant that you had to go to jail."

"Jail?" Burns asked. "What do you mean about jail?"

Bunni brushed her cheeks with the back of her right hand. "Well, that policeman asked me things about you. He said something like, 'That Dr. Burns you work for has a way of turning up at strange times.' And then he asked me if I knew anything about you and Dean Elmore, so I just *had* to tell him."

"Tell him *what*, Bunni?" Burns asked. He had no idea what she could have said that would get her so upset.

"I had to tell him that just on the Friday before Dean Elmore got killed you called him the"—Bunni choked back a sob—"the 'Dear Departed.' "

Burns sank back in his chair. He had completely forgotten that phrase, and he certainly would never have thought that Bunni had such a retentive memory. She had never demonstrated such a facility with memorizing departmental

114

tasks. "Surely you realize it was just a joke," he said.

Bunni sniffed and gave her cheeks another swipe.

Burns opened his bottom desk drawer, took out a family-size box of yellow Puffs, and set it on the front of his desk where Bunni could reach it. She pulled one out, dabbed at her eyes, and blew her nose.

"I thought it was *prob*ably a joke," she said. "But then he was k-k-killed." She grabbed another Puff and worked on her eyes again. They were quite red when she looked up. "I had to tell him about the list, too," she said.

"The list?"

"That one you were writing when I came in last Friday," Bunni said. "The one of things you hate. You wrote Dean Elmore's name on it, and then you stuck it in your desk drawer."

"You can read things that are upside down?" Burns couldn't believe it. Most of his students had a certain amount of difficulty in reading things that were printed in the normal fashion. Bunni was revealing hidden depths.

"I didn't really mean to," she said. "It's just that you were writing on the list, and I was standing here, and so I just glanced at it, and I couldn't help but see what you were writing." She blew her nose into the yellow Puff.

"It's okay," Burns said, hoping that he was telling the truth. "I don't think Napier really suspects that I had anything to do with Dean Elmore's murder. He just has to check out every angle. Like they do on TV."

Bunni looked hopeful. "You really think that?"

"Of course I do," Burns lied. "Don't worry about it. Here, throw those Puffs in the trash and go wash your face before class. There's absolutely no reason for you to worry. Half the campus thinks that I'm an undercover operative for Napier. He wouldn't arrest one of his own men, would he?"

"You're just trying to make me feel better," Bunni said.

"Don't you believe it," Burns said. "You did the right thing."

"Maybe I feel a little guilty, too," Bunni said. "After all, we were picketing Dean Elmore. It seems like kind of a terrible thing to do when you think about it now."

"Don't think that, either," Burns said. "That man was trying to do away with sports, and you had a perfect right to protest. And I was the one who thought of it, not you."

Bunni stood up. "You're sure you're not mad, then."

"Of course not," Burns said. "You start worrying about Nathaniel Hawthorne and forget this other stuff."

"Okay," Bunni said. "You're sure you're not mad?"

"Of course not. Now go get ready for class."

Bunni went out of the office, and Burns sat at his desk trying to decide whether to call Napier or just forget the whole thing. In the end, he decided to forget it. Even Napier wasn't fool enough to make anything of the list or a casual remark, and one that was intended as a joke besides.

The warning bell had already rung, so Burns gathered up his books and walked to his classroom. On the door of the storage room was a new sign:

PLEASE!
Keep This!!
Door!!!
Locked!!!
MAiD Rose

After talking for fifty minutes about a young man who lost his way in a big city, Burns returned to his office to find a note announcing that all afternoon classes had been cancelled so that all faculty and students could attend the funeral of the late Dean Elmore.

116

Clem strolled into the office behind Burns. "Does this mean that we are required to go?" she asked.

"It does look a little bit that way," Burns said, putting his books down on the desk. "To tell the truth, I wasn't really planning to."

"I don't expect that anyone was," Clem said. "I'm sure that *I* have no regrets about his passing."

Burns looked at Clem, noting as he often did how athletically trim she was. He imagined her with the cut-glass paperclip holder in her hand, gripped like a baseball. He thought about her difficulties with Elmore on the Curriculum Committee . . . Then he shook his head. It just wasn't possible.

"I have no regrets, either," Burns said. "But I suppose I'll go, since it seems to be expected."

Clem sniffed. "Seems like a good reason *not* to go to me. But I may go for the son's sake. I wonder how he's taking this?"

Burns walked over to a window and looked out at the grounds. "Fairly well, I think. He was at the pig-kissing contest, you'll recall. He's a strange kid."

"Just how do you mean that?"

"I don't know," Burns said. "There's something about him . . . I think *fey* is the word I'm looking for."

"I know what you're thinking," Clem said, "but you're dead wrong. Oh, he may walk a little funny, but I sponsor a girl's club. From what I hear, he's as live a wire as we have here on the campus. You can't judge a book—"

"—by looking at its cover. I know. I used to listen to Bo Diddley when I was a kid. Well, it was just an idle thought."

"I imagine more people than you have had it," Clem said. "And I'm sure it grated on Elmore quite a bit."

"It must have, knowing him," Burns said.

"Yes," Clem said. "Well, I'll see you at the funeral, I suppose." She turned and left the office.

Burns thought about going to the history lounge for a cigarette, but instead he sat down at his desk and got a clean

117

sheet of paper from one of the drawers. It was time to start a new list.

He uncapped his Pilot Precise Ball Liner and wrote across the top of the page, *People Who Had A Good Reason To Kill Elmore*. Underneath, he wrote the names:

Mal Tomlin: Elmore tried to dump him from the chairmanship and put Clark Woods in.

Clem: Elmore tried to get her fired.

Abner Swan: Elmore delighted in humiliating him at faculty meetings and at the Friday luncheons.

Coach Thomas: Elmore rode him unmercifully about the football team and was planning to do away with the sports program at HGC.

Dorinda Edgely: Elmore might beat her in the pig-kissing contest.

With the last name, Burns capped his pen and tossed it back into the drawer. The reasons he'd jotted down were so far-fetched that what Bunni had told Napier would make *him* a better suspect than nearly any of the people whose names were on the page. And Burns was sure that he hadn't killed Elmore. Changing his earlier decision, he decided to call Napier.

Burns's hand was almost on the beige telephone when it rang, causing him to jerk back reflexively as if he'd grabbed a hot iron bar. Then he picked it up. "Carl Burns," he said into the mouthpiece.

"Verne?"

"That's my cousin Jules. This is Carl Burns. Is that you, Chief Napier?"

"Right. Napier here. I want to talk to you, Verne."

"I'm right here in the office," Burns said. "Come on by."

"That's all right," Napier said. "We can do this on the phone. I'm just calling as a little courtesy. I talked to that little secretary of yours. Honey?"

"Bunni," Burns told him.

"Whatever. Anyhow, she told me about that list of yours and that remark you passed about the 'Dear Departed.' "

"I know," Burns said. "She told me."

"Figured she would. But I don't want you to worry about it. I know you didn't do it despite the fact that you got caught sneaking around the building last night."

"I wasn't sneaking," Burns said. "I was merely . . ."

"Doesn't matter," Napier said. "I never really thought you had anything to do with it. Most English teachers, they're a little too wimpy for a thing like murder. I remember this guy we had in high school. One day we shoved his desk out in the hall and down a flight of stairs. He never even tried to find out who did it. He knew what we'd do if he bothered us . . . But that's not what I called about. I just wanted to say that we've got our man."

Burns was straining not to make some remark about wimps. "Who's the man? What man?"

"Our killer," Napier said. "We've got him."

"So who is it?"

"Coach Thomas," Napier said.

"I don't believe it," Burns said. "Has he admitted anything?"

"Not yet," Napier said. "But he will."

Burns thought about Napier's reputation. He hoped that Coach Thomas wasn't going to find out whether it was based on fact or not. "And you called just to tell me this?"

"Well, there is one other little thing."

"And what might that be?"

"He keeps asking to talk to you," Napier said. "I thought maybe you could come down to the jail—have a little chat with him. Maybe you can save us some trouble."

"I'll talk to him," Burns said. "But I'm not going to get your confession for you."

"Don't be so touchy," Napier said. "You don't have to come at all."

Burns looked at his watch. It was a little after noon, and

119

the funeral wasn't until two o'clock. "I'll be there in fifteen minutes," he said.

13

MAYBE I *AM* a wimp, Burns thought, as he started his Plymouth and drove to the police station. On the other hand, he hadn't felt especially wimpy when he was creeping around in the dark attic of Main the other night. Napier was probably trying to get on his nerves.

The Pecan City jail was not far from the HGC campus, only about a mile and a half. It was a large stone building that had once been white. Now the surface was more of a dingy gray, even black in spots. It needed a good sandblasting job, but the city fathers didn't really see the need for a beautiful jail.

There was a parking lot beside the building, and Burns's tires crunched on the white gravel as he pulled in. He parked his car between a Toyota pickup and a Subaru station wagon. The '67 Plymouth looked like a behemoth beside them. Burns liked that. He hoped the car would never wear out. It had over 130,000 miles on the odometer now, but it showed no signs of old age.

Burns entered the jail building through the front door, which opened into a small room paneled in dark wood. The ceiling seemed extremely low, and Burns had a feeling of being caged in, even though this was an office. The officer at the scarred desk near the door directed Burns to a door that opened into a long hall lined with other doors. He walked down the hall until he came to a door that had a sign on it saying CHIEF R. M. "BOSS" NAPIER. There was a smaller sign underneath, this one hand printed on an index card. It said Enter Without Knocking.

Burns entered.

Napier was sitting behind a desk not nearly as nice as the one Burns had recently left in his own office at HGC, this one being of some blond wood now defaced by numerous scratches, tubular cigarette burns, and marks that had apparently been made by the soles of black shoes. There was a window at Napier's back. It was not barred. Burns had noticed from the outside that the barred windows were on the second and third floors.

The top of Napier's desk was not neat. It was covered with papers, paper clips, note pads, and several account and ledger books. There was even a paperback copy of *Kiss Me, Deadly* sticking out from a pile of federal "wanted" posters. Along the wall to Burns's left there were four iron-gray filing cabinets, with none of the drawers labeled. The walls reminded Burns of the walls in Rogers's office: they were hung with photos of Napier shaking hands with various people, but whereas Burns had known some of the people in Rogers's pictures, he knew none of these. Most of them were wearing a uniform of one kind or another.

The only item of furniture in the room besides Napier's desk, chair, and filing cabinets was a battered straight-backed wooden chair of the same blond wood as the desk. Burns sat in it when Napier invited him to have a seat.

"So you've decided to have a little talk with your buddy, the coach," Napier said.

"Yes," Burns said, "but not to hear his confession or anything like that."

"No need for you to," Napier said, leaning forward and resting his elbows on the desk top. "As soon as we find the murder weapon, he'll crack open like a bad egg."

"You haven't got the weapon?"

"Not yet, but it's just a matter of time. We've got a warrant to search his house."

"His house?" Burns said. "Why would he take it home? You think he kept it as a souvenir?"

Napier stood up. "Don't try to get my goat. I don't care if he threw it in the city dump. We'll find it, and then he'll have to confess."

Burns's mind seized on the image of Coach Thomas in a small, dank dungeon with Napier standing over him while wielding a rubber hose, or perhaps a battery cable.

Napier must have noticed the look on Burns's face. "Don't worry," he said. "We're not going to hurt your pal. We don't have to do things like that anymore. You'd be surprised how most people are affected by just a few days in jail, especially if they've never been in one before."

"I can imagine," Burns said.

"Yeah, I bet you can." Napier stood up. "You want to see him now?"

Burns also stood. "Yes," he said. "Let's go."

Napier took Burns to the second floor by way of a narrow, dimly lighted staircase that reminded Burns of the ones he'd sometimes had to take in hotels when he got tired of waiting for the elevator. They emerged in a short hall with a wooden door on either side. There was a small window set into each door. At the opposite end of the hall there was a heavy door of iron or steel bars. A man in uniform sat on a stool by the door.

Napier opened the door to the room on their right. "Wait in here. We'll bring the coach down to see you."

Burns entered the room. There was a wooden table about the size of a card table and made of the same blond wood as the furniture in Napier's office. The city must have gotten a carload deal of some kind. There were also three of the straight-backed wooden chairs. Burns pulled one of them over to the table and sat down. The table top was covered with cigarette burns and what Burns took to be typical jailhouse graffiti: "If you can't do the time, don't do the crime," "Innocent until proved quilty"—Burns particularly liked that one, and wondered if the prisoner who wrote it simply

123

couldn't spell or if he really meant 'quilty'—and "Aryan Brotherhood." Someone had drawn a line through the latter phrase and printed "Texas Mafia" underneath it, along with a blood-dripping dagger. The walls of the room were dirty, but there was nothing written on them. There was nothing else in the room except an institutional-sized can that had once held something like green beans. Burns assumed that it was there to serve as an ashtray or a cuspidor. All in all, the room reminded him of the history lounge, except that the ceiling was much lower.

The door opened again and Coach Thomas came in, followed closely by Boss Napier. "I'll leave you two alone," Napier said. "Just knock on the door when you're through." He went back out, closing the door behind him.

Thomas's face was drawn, and he was wearing some sort of green twill jumpsuit, which Burns assumed was what the well-dressed inmate wore. He sat in a chair at the table with Burns.

"Well, Coach," Burns said, attempting a light tone, "how'd you get into this mess?"

"It's my own fault," Thomas said. "They heard about something I did, and they already suspected me because of the sports thing." His voice was dry and hesitant, a far cry from the confident voice that Burns had usually heard from him.

"What did they hear?" Burns asked. "That business in the faculty dining room? I've already told Napier that there was nothing to that."

Thomas shook his head. "It's not that. At least that's not all of it."

"What, then?" Burns asked.

"I called Elmore, the night before he was killed."

"What's wrong with that?" Burns asked. "Anybody can call someone on the telephone."

"You don't understand," Thomas said. "It was after the pep rally that the students had. I was really fired up by it, you

124

know? That's about the biggest show of school spirit I've seen since I've been at HGC."

The students at HGC weren't known for their support of the school's athletic program, and that was a fact. Many of them preferred to go home on the weekends, or to make the long drive into Fort Worth and Dallas, rather than to stay in Pecan City and see the football team go down in defeat. "I know what you mean," Burns said.

"So I guess I got excited. I called Elmore up and told him what I thought about him. I told him that he couldn't kill the athletic program and that I'd fight him to keep it. I think I told him that there was no way the program wouldn't go on."

"I still don't see anything wrong," Burns said.

Coach Thomas looked at the ceiling and then at the walls. "I think it was at about that point in the conversation when he said something like 'That football program will go on over my dead body.' "

"Oh," Burns said.

"Yeah. And then I may have called him a few names."

"Names?"

"Yeah. Like maybe 'asshole.' "

"I'll go along with that," Burns said.

"I think maybe I called him a pig, too," Thomas said with a sigh.

"Oh!" Burns said.

"Yeah," Thomas said.

Burns leaned back in his chair. Thomas crossed his arms. The two men sat there like that for several minutes, neither looking at the other.

Then Burns leaned forward. "Just a second," he said. "Who told Napier all this? Surely you didn't."

"No," Thomas said. "It wasn't me. I was just fired up by the pep rally, like I said. It was like in a big game—you never know what you might say in the heat of the moment. Anyway, I'd forgotten all about it until Napier showed up at my house and arrested me."

125

"Well, if you didn't tell him, who did?"

"I figure there was only one person who could've told him," Thomas said. "That kid of Elmore's. What's his name? Wayne? He must've been at home and overheard the phone call. Maybe Elmore even talked to him about it."

"You're probably right," Burns said. "So. What do you want me to do? You must have had a reason for calling."

Thomas looked a little sheepish. "I thought you might talk to Napier, tell him what it was like. Tell him I didn't mean anything by what I said. Maybe you could even talk to that Wayne, tell *him* how it was. That it was just a way of talking." He thought for a minute. "The guy was a pig, though. Even if he is dead, that doesn't change it."

"I doubt that Napier will listen to me very hard or very long," Burns said. "You have a lawyer?"

"I called Tom Dillon, the guy who represents the school," Thomas said. "I don't know if he's done much criminal work. He came and talked to me. He said he'd have me out pretty quick. They don't have much evidence."

"That's true," Burns said. "In fact, they don't have *any* evidence, not to speak of. Just that phone call, and the fact that you and Elmore appeared to have a little tussle at the luncheon last week. Dillon's right. You'll be out of here in no time."

Thomas didn't appear to be cheered up. "I don't know," he said. "Whoever reported that 'little tussle' must've made it look pretty much like a real battle."

"That's only one side of it," Burns said. "Don't worry. You'll be home by tonight."

"You really think so?"

"Sure. Meanwhile, I'll do what I can."

"Thanks, Carl. I appreciate that." Thomas put out his huge hand and the two men shook. Burns went and knocked on the door.

Napier wasn't interested in what Burns had to tell him.

"Look," he said. "He threatened Elmore, and Elmore's dead. He called him a pig, and we got a pig snout on the desk. Before that, he knocked Elmore over in the lunch room."

"But what about evidence?" Burns asked. "You've got to have evidence."

"*I'm* the cop," Napier said. "You're the English teacher. You stick to Bay-o-Wolf and that stuff. I'll catch the bad guys."

"Right," Burns said.

Burns had time for a quick trip to the Taco Bell before going to the funeral. As he washed down his beef tacos with Classic Coke, he realized the irony of the fact that Elmore's funeral was replacing the usual Friday luncheon. Elmore would still be the center of attention. Leave it to him to have the last laugh. So to speak.

Burns parked his car in the lot next to The Church, across the street from Main, and walked up the long, steep cement stairs to the front doors. The Church was a brick building in the style of fifty years ago, which is to say, no style at all. Three sections of wooden pews led down the sloping aisles to the broad platform on which the pulpit stood. Behind the pulpit was the choir loft, and concealed by a discreet curtain in back of the loft was the baptistry. No longer did the devout find it necessary to be immersed in the probably unsanitary waters of Orchard Creek, as Hartley Gorman had been so long ago.

Today, no one really noticed the pulpit or the choir loft or the baptistry. The front of the church was dominated by a large silver and bronze casket, the top portion of which was thrown back to reveal a satiny white lining formed into cushiony billows. The coffin was heaped with wreaths of flowers—mostly carnations—of all colors, and other wreaths were arranged close by on wire stands. Burns wondered who had sent all the flowers, and he strongly suspected that most of them had been paid for by the college.

127

Burns was a little early for the service, having hurried through his tacos. He could still vaguely taste the hot sauce. He stood at the back of the church for a minute, looking over the small group of "mourners" who had gathered so far. Mal Tomlin and Earl Fox were there, along with their wives. Joynell Tomlin was slowly chewing a piece of gum. Mary Fox, in contrast to her husband, looked fashionable and demure. She was wearing black, and she even had on a small black hat. Burns could see the blue and white of Fox's Dallas Cowboys windbreaker peeking over the top of the pew.

On the front row of pews, reserved for the family, sat Wayne Elmore. Beside him sat the only other person on the row, President Rogers's wife, Susan, who was rarely seen at any school or social function. She was pale and wan, and there were all sorts of rumors about the state of her health. She was said to be a victim of cancer, or maybe it was lupus, or possibly even beri-beri. No one knew for sure, and certainly no one was going to ask. Equally interesting and entertaining were the numerous rumors that speculated on her real relationship with Rogers, sexual and otherwise. But all conclusions were inconclusive.

Clem was there, and Miss Darling. Even Larry, Darryl, and Darryl were there, sitting together in a pew near the front. Burns walked down the aisle and sat by Earl Fox.

They all sat in silence—certainly no one was crying—and listened to the organist play sad hymns about crossing Jordan and answering roll calls Up Yonder and feasting on the manna from a bountiful supply. From where he sat, Burns could see Elmore's face where the undertaker had him displayed in the coffin. Elmore didn't seem to be having a better time than anyone else.

Eventually, Rogers walked out onto the platform and stepped behind the pulpit. He talked about being born to trouble and sparks flying upward and the sun also arising. Burns recalled reading somewhere that the minister at Hemingway's funeral had somehow managed to omit those

128

words when reading from Ecclesiastes. He hoped that the sun wouldn't arise on anyone else exactly like Elmore, at least not at HGC.

When it was over, Burns slipped back down the aisle, avoiding the unctuous undertaker who wanted him to go by and view the body. Burns had seen more of Elmore than he cared to.

Outside the church, Burns stood in the dim November sun and felt the chill creeping past his clothes. He walked over to Main and climbed the stairs to the history lounge. He turned on the light, glancing up at the bare bulb dangling down. Fox showed up fairly soon, having sent his wife on home, and they had a smoke. Bel-Air this time. Fox was thinking of saving the coupons. Neither man had much to say. Burns told Fox about Thomas, and Fox swore loudly (after checking to make sure that the door was solidly shut). Then they went home. They didn't like funerals.

14

ON SATURDAY, BURNS read and worked haphazardly on one of his lists, the one that was composed of the ten best rock and roll songs recorded before 1960. It was a particularly troublesome list, because he could never arrive at an adequate definition of rock and roll. He was never sure whether to include a song by Big Joe Turner or not. But if he didn't, could Bill Halcy and the Comets have their cover version included? And should ballads be on there? They were certainly aimed at a rock and roll audience, but could The Platters really be called a rock and roll group?

Besides, limiting the list to only ten songs was ridiculous. Burns knew that he wanted "I Wonder Why," by Dion and the Belmonts, on any version of the list, but what about Buddy Holly? Probably nearly any song that Holly ever recorded belonged on the list, so how could Burns settle for one or two? Not to mention the problem caused by Elvis Presley, though Burns was more and more convinced that Holly had more good songs.

Worrying about such completely trivial matters kept Burns's mind off events at HGC for quite a few hours. He was interrupted only once, by a call from Coach Thomas. "I'm out," Thomas said. "You were right."

"I told you not to worry," Burns said.

"I know," Thomas said, "but that Napier is still out to get me. I can tell."

"Don't worry about it," Burns said. "He'll settle on someone else."

"I hope so," Thomas said.

After the call, Burns found it hard to get his mind back on his list, so he got out a box of old 45 rpm records and listened to The Falcons doing "You're So Fine" and The Fiestas singing "So Fine," trying to decide if either one or both should go on the list. It didn't help much.

On Sunday, Burns slept late and then watched a meaningless and amateurish football game between the Houston Oilers and the Indianapolis Colts. He was glad he wasn't trying to make a list of the most inept teams in the NFL. It would be a hard choice.

After the game he puttered around in his kitchen and fixed himself some bacon and scrambled eggs, which he ate with picante sauce. The taste of the sauce reminded him vaguely of the meal at the Taco Bell, which reminded him of the funeral. There was something about all the things that he had seen and done, heard and said, since Elmore's death that was nagging at him, but he couldn't identify it.

He finished his bacon and eggs, cleaned up the kitchen, washed the frying pan and his dishes, wiped off the table, and sat on his couch to think. He was a student of literature, or at least he liked to think of himself as one, and as such he was trained to look for patterns in a story, novel, or poem. Once he found a meaningful pattern he could build a logical case for an interpretation of the work.

Life, of course, wasn't like a story, but surely there should be some pattern in the events of the past few days, some pattern that would allow him to make sense of things. He was only a wimpy English teacher, not a cop, but he could reason. He could even remember people's names. Surely there was something . . .

But there wasn't.

At least there was nothing really solid. There was one possibility, but it was something that was *only* a possibility. Something that Napier had overlooked, as usual. But Burns had overlooked it, too, and he was the one who should have thought of it. Napier had no real way of knowing.

132

It wasn't important enough to worry about. He could ask Bunni in the morning. He looked on his bookshelves for an old Raymond Chandler novel and went to bed to read.

On Monday morning, Burns went around to Bunni's desk in the long room in front of Larry, Darryl and Darryl's offices. She was sitting there reading her assignment for Burns's ten o'clock class.

Bunni looked up from the text. "Hi, Dr. Burns," she said.

"Good morning, Bunni. There's something I've been meaning to ask you," he said.

Bunni closed the book, marking the place with her finger. "I hope I didn't get you in trouble with the police." There was a look of real concern in her blue eyes.

"Not a bit," Burns said. "This has to do with when you were picketing Dean Elmore's office."

"Oh," Bunni said, slumping in her chair.

"I know you feel bad about that," Burns said. "But you were doing something you believed in. You had no idea that anyone would kill Elmore."

Bunni didn't say anything.

Burns went on. "I was just wondering. You didn't mention it, but were you by any chance still picketing on Tuesday before assembly?"

Bunni removed her finger from the book and put the book on top of a black looseleaf notebook. "Yes," she said. "We were."

"I thought you might have been," Burns said. "I guess you waited until nearly time for assembly to begin before you left."

"We thought he might come out and see the signs," Bunni said. "But he didn't."

Burns didn't think it would be tactful to mention that Elmore, being dead, would have had a great deal of difficulty getting out of the building to see the picket signs.

"Anyway," Bunni said, "we waited till we thought

133

everybody was out, and then we went on to assembly."

"I wondered if you happened to notice anyone go into the building, anyone that you didn't see come out," Burns said.

"Gosh, Dr. Burns, that was a long time ago," Bunni said. "We weren't really looking to see who went in."

"Just think about it for a minute," Burns said. "Maybe something will come to you."

Bunni thought about it. "You know," she said, "I did notice somebody, now that you mention it. I thought it was pretty strange for her to be going in the Administration Building. I don't think I've ever seen her outside of *this* building."

"I knew you could remember," Burns said. "Who was it?"

"It was Miss Darling."

"Miss Darling?"

"That's right. George and I have wondered sometimes how she even makes it up these stairs once a day, but I guess she had to do it twice that day, didn't she?"

"I guess she did," Burns said. He was thinking of sitting in Miss Darling's office the day of the murder. He was thinking about moving her purse, and about how heavy it had felt. As heavy as if it had been concealing a cut-glass paper-clip holder.

"Well, thanks, Bunni," Burns said. He started back to his own office.

"That's all you wanted to know?"

"That's all," Burns said, wondering what Philip Marlowe would do. He went back to his office and got ready for his American lit class.

After class, Burns went down to the history lounge. Fox was already there, tapping Bel-Air ashes into a Sprite can. He pulled the pack out of his pocket and handed it to Burns. "Some funeral, huh?" he said as Burns lit up.

"I guess so," Burns said. "Tell me something. How long has Miss Darling been on the faculty here?"

134

"Forever," Fox said.

"Seriously," Burns said.

"I don't know," Fox said. "I guess we could look in the catalog."

"You have one in your office?"

"Yeah. I'll get it." Fox balanced what was left of his cigarette on the Sprite can and went out. In a minute he was back with the *HGC Bulletin*. He handed it to Burns.

Burns opened the catalog to the back, where the faculty members were listed, and ran his finger down the first page. "Here she is," he said. He showed Fox the details:

DARLING, Alma Sue. *Associate Professor of English*. BA, Baylor, 1938. MA, Baylor, 1939. *Tenured*.

"Tenured!" Fox said. "Tenured! I can't believe this. And she's an associate professor! But she doesn't even have her doctorate! What's going on here?"

Burns knew what Fox meant. It was a well-known fact that no one at HGC had received tenure in the last fifteen years. Whenever there was to be a visit by an accrediting agency, the school's administrators would appoint a committee of faculty to study the matter and to recommend a tenure policy. Then, after the members of the agency's investigative team had left the campus, the administration would reject the policy, in fear that if too many people got tenure there would be no way to fire anyone in case of severe financial crunch. But Miss Darling was a special case.

"Don't you remember that faculty meeting about ten years ago?" Burns asked. "We were both pretty new here, and President Rogers got up and announced that he was giving Miss Darling tenure just because he wanted to and because she served as president of the Faculty Club?"

Fox slid his Bel-Air into the Sprite can and lit another one. "I remember now," he said. "We couldn't believe it. Of course, I'd believe anything now. It didn't take long to get used to stuff like that."

"I guess that's how she got to be an associate, too," Burns said.

"It must be nice," Fox said. "Alma Sue. Can you beat that?"

"I wouldn't even try," Burns said. "See you later." He left the lounge and went back upstairs.

In his office, Burns began trying to fit things into a pattern. Miss Darling, who was slightly flaky anyway, must feel an intense loyalty to the school that had given her a promotion that, according to the rules, she really didn't merit. Not only that, she had received tenure, something that no one else had accomplished in fifteen years. And here was Elmore, running the school straight into bankruptcy. Of course, Miss Darling had never spoken out in faculty meetings. That wouldn't be her style. But no doubt she had seen what was going on, and it worried her. The final blow must have been Elmore's plan to make the school a sort of degree mill. Miss Darling had gone to see him, probably only to discuss the situation. Something had been said, heated words exchanged, and Miss Darling had snatched up the paper-clip holder and lashed out at Elmore with it, not realizing that she was striking a blow that could kill.

The more Burns thought about his reconstruction of events, the more plausible it seemed. But what about the pig's snout?

All right, assume that Dorinda Edgely (and why wasn't *she* at the funeral?) actually had lost the snout in the ladies' room in Main. Miss Darling could have seen it there and picked it up easily enough. Maybe she was thinking of returning it. Or maybe she thought that Elmore was a pig for what he was doing to HGC. Anyway, she took the snout with her to his office and left it there rather than try to retrieve it from beneath his head after striking him.

It was all plausible. It all fit. But Burns realized that he had really done exactly the same thing that Napier had done with Coach Thomas: he had built a fine tissue of assumptions and possibilities, without a single piece of factual evidence to support them.

Burns thought again about Miss Darling's purse and how heavy it had been. Surely by now she would have managed to dispose of the paper-clip holder. But where had she put it? She wouldn't think like a criminal and throw it off the nearest bridge over Orchard Creek, surely. What if she'd hidden it somewhere in her office?

Of course, assuming she did carry the weapon out of the building in her purse, she could simply have taken it home and put it out with the trash. Every block in Pecan City had a large metal dumpster situated in the alley behind the houses. Twice a week, the city's garbage trucks came by and hoisted up the dumpsters, pouring the contents into a large bin and crushing them before taking everything to the sanitary landfill, where it was dumped into a hole and covered with dirt by a bulldozer.

If Miss Darling had disposed of the cut-glass weapon that way, there was little chance that it would ever be seen again; and Burns thought that if he had been in possession of something that he had used to kill someone, he would get rid of it in just that way.

But Miss Darling might not have been thinking clearly. The killing might have rattled her, and she might have done something foolish, like hiding the holder in her office.

Burns decided to search her office.

He realized that he was working on only one piece of information, the fact that Bunni had seen Miss Darling enter the Administration Building shortly before assembly. He knew that he wouldn't let a student get by with that sort of reasoning in an essay. But it all seemed so possible.

Miss Darling never went to lunch, probably because she didn't want to have to walk down the stairs and then return. She always brought a sandwich and ate it in her office. Then

137

she remained there, keeping office hours, until exactly two o'clock every afternoon.

Burns puttered around his office, waiting for her to leave. He worked on an essay test for his American literature class and read some more Faulkner articles for his Tuesday night class. He was going to dazzle them with his knowledge of *The Sound and the Fury* this week. He just hoped that most of them, or even some of them, had read it. There was always a run on the bookstore's supply of *Cliff's Notes* when he started on Faulkner.

Finally two o'clock came. Burns heard Miss Darling's door close and lock with a precise little click. The third floor was so shaky that he could feel the vibrations as she walked to the stairs. He waited until he thought she had had plenty of time to reach the ground floor. He was reasonably sure that she wouldn't be coming back up. As far as he knew, she never had.

Burns walked to Miss Darling's door. As chairman of the department, he had a master key, in case one of the instructors was ill and he needed access to an office, or in case he needed to get in for some other emergency. He had never used the key for snooping before, and he felt slightly guilty about doing so this time, but after only a slight pause he slipped the key into the lock. It went in smoothly. He turned it to the left and opened the door, slipping quietly inside.

Closing the door behind him, Burns flipped on the light switch. Miss Darling's office was as neat as she was. On the desk were a calendar, a picture of Miss Darling's cat, and nothing else. Burns, whose own desk was usually cluttered with papers, notes, pens, and books, thought that it was the neatest teacher's desk he'd ever seen. The books on the wall of shelves beside the desk were equally neat, arranged by size rather than in alphabetical order. Small books were with small books, large with large. Burns wondered how Miss Darling ever found anything.

The neatness would certainly make the office easy to

search. In fact, there was nowhere to look except in the desk drawers. Burns was about to step around in front of the desk and search it when the door opened at his back.

Burns was humiliated. He could feel the back of his neck getting warm, and the blood was gathering in his ears. Clem's office door had been closed, and he had assumed that she was gone. Either he'd been wrong, or Miss Darling had returned.

Burns turned slowly around.

"I swear, Doctah Burns, what *you* doin' in here?" Rose asked. "Is Miss Darlin' been leavin' her doah open, too?" Rose stood there with her hands on her hips, looking at Burns. He could see the vacuum cleaner in the hall beyond her.

"I . . . I, uh, yes. Yes. I noticed that the door wasn't quite closed, so I looked in to see if Miss Darling was still here." Burns wiped his hand across his upper lip. "She usually leaves about this time, but I wanted to ask her about a committee assignment, so I stepped in."

"Well, she better start lockin' her doah," Rose said. "Too much funny business goin' on around here."

"Yes," Burns said. "Well, I think I'll be going back to my own office now. You can lock up when you're through."

"I'll do that. You can sure bet I'll do that," Rose said.

Burns eased by her and out the door. Her powerful sloping shoulders, no doubt a result of years of dragging the vacuum cleaner up the stairs of Main, made her look like a much more likely murderer than Miss Darling would ever be. If he hadn't been so intent on searching the office, Burns thought, he would surely have heard her coming.

"Ain't nevah lef' a doah unlocked in all my life," Rose said as Burns reached the hall. "Nevah have, nevah will. Say 'Rose, you lef' that doah unlocked' all they want, don't mean I did it. No, sir."

Burns wasn't sure whether he was being addressed or whether Rose was talking to herself, so he sidled down the

139

hall and back to his own office. He was both embarrassed and ashamed, embarrassed to have been caught snooping, and ashamed to have been snooping in the first place.

Still, there was the nagging thought that he just might be right about Miss Darling. He decided to snoop again, but later. After everyone, including Rose, had gone home.

By a little after five o'clock, Burns was convinced he was alone in the building. The feeling of emptiness with which he was so familiar had settled over the third floor, having worked its way up from the ground.

Once more Burns entered Miss Darling's office. He didn't pause to look around but instead went straight to the desk and pulled open the thin middle drawer. It was as neat as the top of the desk. Typing paper was in one stack, notebook paper in another. There was a grade book and an assortment of pens. That was all.

The desk was not as large as the one in Burns's office, having only three drawers on one side. Burns opened the top one. Index cards, note pads, a box of paper clips, a stapler, a box of staples. That was all.

Burns opened the second drawer. Student essays, neatly stacked and held in groups by red rubber bands. Nothing else.

The third drawer was equally neat and equally unproductive. It contained thin stacks of lecture notes, written in a dedicated, crabbed hand on yellow legal-sized paper. Burns picked them up and looked at them out of mild curiosity, but not seeing any lists he put them back down.

There was nowhere else to look. Burns went back to his own office and sat down. He stared at the rows and rows of books on his own shelves; they were arranged more or less according to subject and therefore didn't have the neat appearance of Miss Darling's. *Myths of the Greeks and Romans, The Greek Way, The Roman Way. Love and Death in the American Novel, Studies in Classic American Literature, The*

140

American Novel and its Tradition. Burns liked to look at the spines and think about the contents. The books were like old friends to him.

He propped his feet up on the desk. He wondered if Miss Darling had ever read *Love and Death in the American Novel*. Probably not. She'd probably never heard of it. Not that he thought that mattered.

Well, he thought, if Miss Darling killed Elmore, I'll never find it out for sure. Let Napier catch her. It's his job, after all. My job is to teach William Faulkner. He picked up *The Sound and the Fury* and started to reread the Benjy section. Soon he was so involved with the problems of the Compson family that he had completely forgotten Miss Darling, Dean Elmore, and the cut-glass paper-clip holder. It was going to be a good class. He was looking forward to Tuesday night.

15

WHEN BURNS ENTERED graduate school in the 1960s, he had
no real idea of what the academic world was like. He had a
vague idea that it was full of gentleman scholars who spent
their spare time debating (in a calm and judicial manner, of
course) the merits of blank verse, or perhaps exchanging
ideas on the identity of the Pearl Poet.

He was completely wrong, as he soon found out. There
was more backbiting, favor-currying, intellectual snobbery,
and intellectual dishonesty than he would have believed had
anyone told him that it existed. The fights for tenure among
faculty members at the school he attended were particularly vicious. As one of his professors had put it, "It's like getting your balls caught in a sewing machine."

And since it was, after all, the 1960s, there was a lot more
going on outside the classrooms than was going on inside
them. It was hard for many professors to get interested in the
environmental themes to be found in the *Leatherstocking
Tales* when the university administration had decided to
bulldoze the trees along Waller Creek. Burns himself hadn't
staged sit-ins in any trees, but several of his professors had.
And several of the graduate students had been a lot more interested in scoring dope than in talking about the distortions
of time in *Catch-22*, while others spent most of their time
marching on the state capitol or protesting the invasion of
Cambodia.

Burns had enjoyed being a part of it all, and he had sailed
through graduate school with the naive idea that if he kept
his nose clean and his hair short, he'd be able to get a job

143

anywhere he chose, and name his own price. He had a vague picture in the back of his mind of walking into the office of the department chairman at, say, Harvard, announcing that he had earned his Ph.D., and being warmly welcomed into the fraternity of scholars. Perhaps the other members of the department would drop by for a little wine and cheese and discuss the effect of Zola on the novels of Frank Norris.

When he got his diploma, after five years of course work, qualifying exams, minor orals, major orals, writing and defending a dissertation, Burns found out how naive he had really been. Not only was he not welcomed at Harvard, he was hardly welcomed anywhere. It seemed as if everyone in the country had, in about 1966, gotten the urge to take a Ph.D. in English. There were hundreds of applicants for every position that opened, and thousands if the position was a particularly good one. Even worse, there were very few positions that opened.

Burns laboriously typed hundreds of letters of application. He studied the *Chronicle of Higher Education* and the MLA's job listings. He began to pay close attention to the obituaries.

From many schools, he received no response at all. From some, he received form letters stating that there were simply no openings. From others, he heard that, while there was indeed an opening, it was not likely to be filled by a graduate of a provincial state university in a provincial state like Texas. One school even sent a long letter listing all the terrible attributes of the city in which it was located, a clever ploy to discourage all but the most determined.

And from some schools, Burns received a favorable response. Most of them were small denominational schools whose personnel officers were probably quite pleased to see the photo of Burns on his vita sheet. They probably didn't get many applicants with short hair in those days, and Burns had often speculated that under more recent conditions, when photos were not included on applications, he might not

144

have gotten a job at all.

Several of his friends *didn't* get jobs, at least not in teaching. One of them had become a technical writer. One was working his way up the management ladder of J. C. Penney's. And one had tried short-order cooking, cab driving, and banking. The last Burns had heard from him, he was selling insurance. Burns had bought a ten-thousand-dollar term policy from him.

The funny thing (to Burns) was that none of his friends envied him his job. They let it be known quite clearly that they would rather have been reduced to running the sewage sifter in the water treatment plant than teach at Hartley Gorman College, their idea of academic purgatory.

Burns didn't mind. He had a job—though it didn't pay very well—doing what he wanted to do, and there was no fight for tenure, since HGC didn't have tenure. He would never become famous for his pronouncements on the first canto of *Don Juan*, and the editors of academic journals might sniff when he sent them articles with HGC as a return address, but he could be satisfied that he was doing a good job of teaching some unworldly students about worldly literature.

Besides, Burns had found friends at HGC. He liked most of his co-workers, particularly Fox and Tomlin, and his departmental duties were not much of a burden. He would never make much money, and even his pension would be small, but he had been forewarned by one of his professors that there was a serpent in every Eden, and that the serpent in denominational schools was money.

Obviously the professor had never known Elmore, a snake if there ever had been one. The dean had driven away the students, alienated the local supporters of the school, and destroyed the morale of the faculty. Even now, deader than the aurochs, he was still stirring the cauldron. Coach Thomas had been thrown in jail, Main had almost been burned, and Burns had become so suspicious of people around him that he'd made a list of people who might have killed Elmore and

145

then let his thinking become so warped that he'd even begun to suspect Miss Darling of the murder.

What really galled Burns was the thought that Elmore would have loved all the confusion and uncertainty. He was six feet under, mouldering in his grave, but he would have loved knowing that his legacy was more chaos for the faculty of HGC.

Burns wondered what it really was that had gotten Elmore killed. Whoever did it must have had a temper to match Elmore's own, or else had been provoked in the extreme. It could never have been Miss Darling, and Burns repented his suspicions of her. He remembered that once, at a faculty meeting, Elmore had gotten so angry that he seemed about to explode. Literally. His face had suffused with blood, his neck had become engorged, and even his ears had seemed to swell. Burns had thought that at any second Elmore might burst with a disgusting pop and spread parts of himself all over the chapel walls and ceiling. It hadn't happened, but it had seemed likely.

The episode had become famous as "The Case of the Locked Door," and it had been Clem who was responsible. She had a student who was habitually ten or fifteen minutes late for class. The girl would straggle in, walk in front of Clem, and betake herself to a seat in the rear of the class. As soon as she was seated and had arranged her books satisfactorily, she would raise her hand and, not waiting for acknowledgment, say something like, "Hey, I'm sorry I'm late, but my ride didn't pick me up on time, you know? Could you go over what I've missed?"

After three weeks of this, Clem announced that she would no longer tolerate latecomers. The girl was late the next day anyway, and the day after that. The day after that, Clem locked the door when the bell rang. Ten or so minutes later there came a tapping, as of someone gently rapping, rapping at the classroom door.

Clem ignored it.

146

The rapping became louder.

Clem continued to ignore it.

The rapping stopped, and Clem figured she had won the battle.

Unfortunately, the girl's father was a contributor to a small scholarship fund. He contributed about fifty dollars a year, which he decided made him one of the school's mainstays. He went directly to Rogers, who sent him to Elmore, who was shocked and appalled that any member of the HGC faculty could be so heartless and irresponsible as to attempt to deny an education—an education that was being bought and paid for—to any student, even one who was "occasionally" late. He had denounced Clem, by name, in the faculty meeting, becoming so exercised in the process that his bursting seemed imminent.

If Bunni had seen Clem coming out of the administration building, Burns would have searched her office in a minute, though he was convinced that Clem was no more a killer than Miss Darling.

All these thoughts occupied Burns's mind for much of Tuesday. He taught his early class, smoked with Fox, visited Mal Tomlin, read a few Faulkner articles, dawdled around waiting for his night class to begin, and generally tried to organize his thoughts about what was going on. He came to no conclusions, and he certainly came up with no new evidence and no new clues. In fact, he was beginning to feel like a total waste.

He felt better after his night class, however. The students had responded to *The Sound and the Fury*. Several of them appeared to have actually read the book, and they appreciated the subtlety of Faulkner's intricate structure, the way the four parts of the book spoke to one another and to the reader. Some of them even planned to read the book again.

All in all, Burns didn't feel too bad about things as he left Main that night.

He started feeling a lot worse when he saw the fire in the Administration Building.

As usual, Burns had parked the Plymouth on the street. That way he didn't have to walk to the parking lot, and he didn't have to worry about getting a ticket for parking in a student space or some other niggling violation that he wouldn't even be aware of committing. He was walking toward the car when he saw the fire. By then, it was already too late.

The weather that day had been dry, and the wind had kicked up from the north once again. It was strong all day, and was still gusting up to twenty- or twenty-five miles an hour, just the kind of wind to really fan some flames if they were going well.

The flames that Burns saw were going well. They were in the attic of the building, and there was no telling how long they had been burning. The Administration Building's attic was windowless, but it had large vent grills on either end. There was no way to see through the vents. Burns wouldn't have seen the flames had they not begun eating their way through the roof.

Burns turned and ran back to Main. He had no key to any office except those on the third floor, so he charged up to the third floor, fumbled with his key, finally got it into the lock, rushed into his office, flipped open the telephone book, got the number of the Pecan City Fire Department, and punched it on the buttons of the beige phone.

"Fire Department," a bored voice answered on the first ring. Pecan City's dispatcher wasn't one of the busiest people in town.

"The HGC Administration Building is on fire," Burns said, as calmly as he could. He was still panting from his charge up the stairs.

The dispatcher perked up. "Name?"

"Dr. Carl Burns. Hurry!" Burns hung up the phone and

148

ran back to the staircase. He had gone only as far as the second floor when he heard the fire siren begin its howling.

The Pecan City Fire Department was not known for its efficiency. The standing joke among most members of the community was that they "usually managed to save the lot, but sometimes they lost the slab." Whether it was lack of practice, Pecan City not having many fires of much consequence, or whether it was simple inability, no one knew. Whatever the reason, Burns held out little hope for the Administration Building. He wished that Elmore were alive to see it—the numbering system was going to be all fouled up.

By the time Burns got back outside, the building's roof was engulfed; fire was licking out the vent under the arch, and now Burns could see flames through the windows of the second floor.

The fire station was only four blocks from the campus, and the trucks arrived almost as soon as Burns heard their wailing. There were three of them, and the drivers slammed them to a halt in front of the burning building. Men dropped off the sides and tops and began hauling hoses to the fireplugs. In a short time, water was rushing through the hoses and gushing through the air. The wind was so strong that it was hard to direct the streams.

Within minutes, all the students living in the dorms had gathered, along with numbers of the curious, drawn by the flames like mindless insects. It was quickly clear to most of them that the building was doomed. There weren't enough fire hydrants, the fire was too far advanced, and the wind had whipped the flames too high. Everyone stood and watched the building burn. No one stood very close. The flames were too hot.

After a while, Burns noticed that there was someone standing next to him. It was Napier. "Hear you called in the alarm," Napier said.

"That's right," Burns said.

"Interesting," Napier said.

149

Burns didn't say anything. There was a loud "O-h-h-h-h-h-h-h!" from the crowd as the roof fell in, carrying most of the second floor along with it to the bottom. There was an explosion of flame and sparks.

"Better than the Fourth of July," Napier said. "Anybody in there, you think?"

"Not at this time of night," Burns said. "Not unless someone was working really late. There aren't any classes in there."

"Too late now, anyway," Napier said.

Burns didn't have anything to say to that, either.

The burning went on for a long time. President Rogers arrived on the scene, and everyone who worked in the building either showed up or was reached by telephone. It appeared that there would be no casualties, except, of course, for the building itself.

Most of the spectators stayed to the bitter end, as Burns did. Even when the fire appeared to be out, the firemen continued to spray water into the ruins. They were afraid of sparks. With the wind so high, it was quite lucky that no other buildings had caught fire. The north wind, however, was blowing only toward the school's tennis courts and a vacant parking lot.

By two o'clock in the morning, it was all over. Just about all that was left of the Administration Building were the blackened walls, and they would have to be knocked down the next day as a safety precaution as soon as the fire marshal had inspected the premises, or what was left of the premises.

As the crowd began to thin out, Burns looked for Rogers. He saw him, standing on the fringes of the lawn, his hands thrust deeply into the pockets of a London Fog overcoat. His round face was set in a deep frown, a far cry from its usual smile.

"I hope we were overinsured," Burns said, half seriously.

Rogers looked at him. "We weren't," he said. "Under, if

150

anything." They both stared gloomily at the walls. Burns imagined that his next year's raise had just gone up in smoke. Literally.

Napier, who had been talking to various members of the crowd, drifted over. "Looks like Burns wasn't able to stop this one," he said.

Burns was momentarily disconcerted that Napier had gotten his name right. "I tried," he said.

"Do you think it might have been the same person?" Rogers said.

"I don't know," Napier said. "Who had keys to this place, except for the people who worked there?"

"No one," Rogers said. He thought for a minute. "Of course, the security staff had keys, and the maintenance crew. No one else."

Burns stifled a laugh. The security staff was Dirty Harry. The maintenance crew was Rose's cousin Nadine. Rogers was a perfect bureaucrat, even in times of stress.

"I'll have to question all of them," Napier said. "Starting at eight o'clock."

"I'll let them know," Rogers said. "We'll have to do it in the cafeteria. I'll have to locate new offices for everyone and . . ." He put a hand to his forehead. "And I don't know what we'll do about the files, the letters, the papers, the . . ." His voice trailed off and he shook his head wearily.

Napier was not someone to go overboard in sympathy. "Well, just have everybody there at eight o'clock. Or most of them. A few stragglers won't matter. Just so we get to see all of them."

"I'll see to it," Rogers said. Then he wandered off.

"You know, Burns," Napier said, "it's interesting that you're *always* around when these things happen."

"I'm sure you don't mean anything by that," Burns said. "And I've been meaning to ask you, what about the man who was watching Main? Why didn't he spot the fire?"

Napier looked chagrined. "Because I pulled him off, that's

151

why. After nothing happened on the weekend, I figured it was all over. I should've waited."

"No way you could have known," Burns said. "You think these fires are tied in to the murder?"

"Ask your friend Thomas," Napier said. "Maybe he could tell you." He turned and walked away. After a few more minutes of looking at the ruins, Burns left, too, hoping for a few hours' sleep before his first class.

16

MOST OF THE students in Burns's eight o'clock class were as sleepy as he was. Somehow, they all struggled through. As soon as the bell rang, Burns headed for the ground floor for a Pepsi. He had to go all the way down, because there were no soft drink machines on any of the other floors. Burns was never sure whether that was because the machines were too heavy to haul up the steep stairs, which had a ninety-degree turn in the middle of the climb, or whether the soft drink companies were afraid that the machines would fall through the floor if somehow they were lugged up the stairs.

He put two quarters into the silver slot on the big blue and white machine and punched the button for a Pepsi. The machine clanked and rattled and eventually deposited a can in the rack. Burns had to turn the can sideways to get it out.

As he peeled off the pull-tab opener, Mal Tomlin walked up. "Not much left of Hartley Gorman II, is there?"

"Not much," Burns agreed. "Want to go up to the history lounge?"

Tomlin nodded, and they went up to look for Fox, who was, as usual, sitting by the dilapidated card table thumping ashes into a soft drink can, this time a red and gold caffeine-free Diet Coke container.

Burns and Tomlin pulled up chairs. Tomlin bummed a smoke from Fox, as did Burns. Bel-Airs again. Soon the room was filling with a smoky haze.

"Who did it?" Fox asked no one in particular. "Rogers," he said, answering his own question. "Rogers did it. Insurance. That's the rumor."

"I don't think there's anything to it," Burns said. "He told me last night that the building was underinsured if anything, so I doubt that he had anything to do with it. Besides, he was called at home and came to the fire."

Tomlin leaned back on two legs of the chair and blew smoke. "Doesn't mean a thing. He could have started the fire, left, and then come back."

"Right," Fox said.

Burns realized that they weren't serious, really, but he kept up the discussion. "Let's look at it this way. Suppose that insurance doesn't have anything to do with it." He tapped his cigarette on the aluminum can. "I admit that I thought the same thing at first, but whoever I saw in the attic upstairs, it certainly wasn't Rogers. I heard his voice, remember, and it wasn't Rogers's voice. I'd recognize that anywhere."

Tomlin brought his chair back to a four-legged position with a thump. "If it wasn't insurance, what was it?"

"I haven't got that part figured out yet," Burns said.

"Once you get past money," Fox said, "there's only two things left: love and hate."

"Uh-oh," Burns said.

Tomlin and Fox looked at him. "What do you mean, 'uh-oh'?" Fox asked.

Burns dumped his butt into the can. "I mean that you're thinking like Napier. I think he's all set to blame this on Coach Thomas, judging from something he said last night. I bet he thinks Thomas did it for revenge."

"Thomas hadn't even been thrown in jail by the time of the first fire," Tomlin said. "So where's the revenge?"

Burns thought about it. "No one said that both fires had to be set by the same person."

"You sort of implied that yourself," Fox said, "But so what? Let's keep this simple and assume that there's only one firebug loose on the campus at any given time. Thinking about two would be too much of a strain."

154

"How about thinking that there's a murderer and a firebug loose at the same time?" Tomlin asked. "Are we thinking about one person, two, or three?"

"This is too complicated," Burns said. No one disagreed with him.

"I have a confession to make," Burns said after a minute or two had gone by in silence.

"So confess," Fox said.

"I made a list of people I thought might have had a reason for killing Elmore. Both of you were on it."

"I'd have been disappointed if you'd left me off," Fox said. "Have another smoke." He tossed the nearly empty Bel-Air pack to Burns.

Burns shook out a cigarette. "I have another confession to make," he said.

"My God, you didn't give the list to Boss Napier, did you?" Tomlin asked.

Burns lit up. "It's not that bad. It's just that . . . for a little while . . . I thought maybe Miss Darling had killed Elmore."

"Good grief," Fox said. "All this mess is getting to you. Maybe you ought to take a day or two of personal leave."

"It's not that bad," Burns said. "I got over the idea pretty quickly."

"At least you're not completely crazy," Tomlin said. "You just need a little more smoke in your lungs and you'll be fine."

Burns looked at the high ceiling of the history lounge. A thin white cloud hovered a foot or two below it. He laughed. "Anyone who walked in here and took a deep breath would be in danger of contracting emphysema," he said. He dumped his Bel-Air in the Coke can. "I've got to go teach a class."

"Me, too," Tomlin said. They left Fox sitting in the smoke-filled room.

Burns talked for an hour about Emerson, giving the class a list of the characteristics of American Transcendentalism

155

to study for their next test, but his mind was on Miss Darling. As foolish as the idea of her killing Elmore seemed, the fact remained that Bunni had seen her go into the building shortly before assembly on the day Elmore was killed. And it was a fact that Miss Darling *never* left the third floor of Main before her teaching day was over. And Miss Darling could have picked up the pig snout in the ladies' room. And her purse *had* been awfully heavy . . . Burns decided that he would have a talk with Miss Darling.

After class, he avoided the crowd of students and hurried to his office. Then he called Miss Darling and asked her to step in. "Right away, Dr. Burns," she said.

She came into Burns's office wearing her blue suit with the huge bow at the neck, one of about four outfits that she alternated throughout the year. "Wasn't it just terrible, Dr. Burns?"

"Yes," Burns said. "Terrible. Uh . . . wasn't *what* terrible?"

"The fire, of course. Oh, I'm afraid that it will take us years to get all straight again. Why, wherever will they find offices for everyone?"

Burns felt off balance. This wasn't exactly the way he'd planned for the conversation to go. "I don't know," he said. "But I'm sure that Dr. Rogers will take care of everything."

"Oh, I'm sure he will," Miss Darling said. "It just seems so . . . so . . ."

"Yes," Burns said. "It does. But there's something I need to ask you, Miss Darling."

Miss Darling's gaze cleared, as if she realized for the first time that it was Burns who had called her and not the other way around. "Certainly, Dr. Burns. Whatever you say."

"I'd like to ask you a question about the day Dean Elmore was killed."

"Oh, my." Miss Darling, who had been standing in front of Burns's desk, plopped into one of the chairs and folded her hands in her lap.

"You see," Burns said in a voice as kind as he could make it, "a student happened to mention to me that you were seen going into the Administration Building shortly before Dean Elmore died."

"Oh, my," Miss Darling said again.

"So I thought that perhaps you . . . uh, might have seen something suspicious, or some*one* suspicious if you were there."

"Oh, my," Miss Darling repeated.

Burns was beginning to wonder if she had slipped into permanent senility. Her vocabulary certainly seemed to have become suddenly limited. "*Did* you see anyone?" he asked.

"Oh, my," Miss Darling said.

Burns stood up and came around his desk to stand by her chair. "Are you all right, Miss Darling?"

She looked up at him, then back down. "Yes," she said.

It wasn't much, but it was an improvement. "Then can you answer the question? It's only for me, not for the police."

She looked up again, fearfully this time. "Oh, I could never talk to the police! I . . . I'm very afraid of the police." Her folded hands clasped one another in her lap.

Burns walked back behind his desk and sat down. "Of course not," he said. "You wouldn't have to. It's just that I'm curious." He leaned back in his chair and tried to look relaxed.

"I didn't see anyone," she said, very quietly.

Burns tried not to lean forward, but he did anyway. "You were there, then? In the Administration Building?"

"Yes." Miss Darling's voice was by now barely audible.

Burns resisted the temptation of asking her to speak up. "Why?"

"Well," Miss Darling said, "I had found the pig's snout in the ladies' room, and it reminded me of Dean Elmore."

So I was right, Burns thought.

"I remembered how much he enjoyed the contest each year," Miss Darling went on. "So I picked it up. But then I

157

thought about how angry I was with his proposal to grant those degrees to people who hadn't even taken any course work. I thought I'd go and tell him about it, and I took the snout with me."

Sort of right, at least, Burns thought.

"He was *very* rude to me," Miss Darling said, her voice gaining strength. "He said . . . he said that I was old and behind the times, that perhaps it was time for me to move on. He said that I didn't know a thing about what was meant by 'modern education.' He said that the academic world had passed me by."

"That was certainly unkind," Burns said, hating himself for having had similar feelings.

"I told him that if he stood for modern education, then I was glad not to know about it," Miss Darling said with more spirit than Burns had credited her with. "I told him that I could still recognize a good sentence when I saw one, and a good paragraph, too. And that most of my students could when they finished one of my courses. I told him that I could still recite the first forty-two lines of *The Canterbury Tales*, and that if modern education was opposed to that, then I didn't think much of modern education."

"Well," Burns said.

"Yes," Miss Darling said. "And then I threw the pig's snout on his desk and left the office."

"I wonder why I didn't see you on my way over," Burns said.

"Oh," Miss Darling said, "that's simple. I decided that since I was already downstairs, I'd go to assembly. I went out the back door."

After Miss Darling had left, Burns thought about what she'd told him. It was all possible, and it explained the snout, which wasn't a comment after all, or not a direct one. He had forgotten the back door. The Administration Building had originally served as the school's library, and the back

158

entrance was not convenient. It had been designed for use by the library employees, not for anyone who might be trying to sneak out with an unchecked book or magazine, and most students and newer faculty members probably didn't even know how to get to it. But Miss Darling knew, and the killer could have known as well, which would explain why no one had passed Burns as he went into the building.

Burns had no intention of telling Napier what he'd learned. Let the police chief work it out for himself. Miss Darling, he was convinced, was guilty of absolutely nothing, and two minutes with Napier would probably reduce her to a substance resembling Jell-O Instant Pudding.

Burns was happy to have solved the mystery of the snout, but he was no closer to finding out who was responsible for the murder of Elmore, or for the fire. Philip Marlowe would be ashamed of him. He thought about forgetting the whole thing, but then he remembered Napier's remark about his being a "wimpy English teacher," or words to that effect. He decided not to forget the whole thing.

Besides, he hadn't done too badly. He knew something Napier didn't know, and he had been at least as right as Napier about the possibility of a second attempt to burn Main. He'd had the wrong building, that's all; but so had Napier.

He tried to think what Philip Marlowe would do next. After a while, he reached for the telephone and called Wayne Elmore.

Elmore and his son had lived together in a white frame house in the older residential area of Pecan City. The house was well kept-up, and it had been painted within the last two or three years. It was surrounded by huge pecan trees, and there was a wide yard of St. Augustine grass, most of which was brown now. There hadn't been a really hard freeze, however, so there were still a few patches of green to be seen. Desiccated brown leaves covered much of the yard.

Burns parked his Plymouth and walked up the walk to the front porch. There was even a wooden swing suspended from the porch ceiling by chains hanging from two hooks. There was no doorbell, and Burns knocked on the door frame beside the screen door.

Wayne Elmore opened the inner door almost at once.

"Hello, Wayne," Burns said. "I'm Carl Burns. I called a little while ago."

"Come in, Dr. Burns," Wayne said. His voice was light and breathy. He moved back from the door, opening it all the way in, as gracefully as a dancer.

Burns pulled open the screen and went inside. The house looked as if it had been furnished when it was built. There was a couch covered with a large floral print, a Duncan Phyfe coffee table with a glass top, two uncomfortable-looking wooden chairs with plump cloth-covered seats and inserts in their backs, and a large wooden art-deco floor lamp, its shade hung with heavy tassels. The hardwood floor was covered with throw rugs in front of the chairs. There was another rug on which the coffee table stood.

Wayne glided over to one of the chairs and sat down, neatly crossing one leg over the other. "What can I do for you, Dr. Burns?" he asked in his affected voice.

Without being asked, Burns sat on the couch. He was already beginning to regret having come. He had no idea why he was here, really. It was stupid to play detective if you didn't know what you were doing. Still, he was here, so he might as well see it through. "I'm sorry about your father, Wayne," he said.

"Thank you," Wayne replied. "I'm sure you mean that sincerely." He clasped his hands and hooked them over his knee.

Burns had not expected sarcasm. He decided to go along with it. "You're right, of course," he said. "I'm being hypocritical. Maybe I meant that I'm sorry for you. I know it must be hard."

160

"Ha. What do you know about it? You don't know the half of it, Dr. Burns." Wayne's voice took on a harder edge.

"I'm sorry. I . . ."

"Don't say it." Wayne unclasped his hands, uncrossed his legs, and leaned forward. "You're a hypocrite, all right, just like all the rest of them at that school. You come here pretending to be sympathetic, but you're not. You just want to throw more dirt. My father had more dirt thrown on him while he was alive than was thrown on his coffin after he died. And all of it was thrown by the good Christians at Hartley Gorman College. What a laugh!"

"That's not why I came, Wayne, not at all." Burns was feeling defensive now. "I simply wanted to ask if you knew of anyone who might have benefited from killing your father."

"You're trying to make me laugh again," Wayne said. "Please don't do that. I know you hated him. I know you all hated him. Do you think I didn't hear all the talk from the students? Sure, they all avoided me like I had cholera, but I heard. I got the message." He got up from the chair and walked over to where Burns sat.

"You want to know who killed my father? You did, and all the rest of the sanctimonious hypocrites at that school! You all killed him!" Wayne's voice rose, and he pointed his finger straight at Burns.

Burns was feeling as uncomfortable as he could remember ever having felt. He wanted to get up and leave, but he couldn't. Wayne was standing in his way. "I wish you didn't feel that way, Wayne. It's true—"

"It's true that you killed him!" Wayne said, his voice rising. "Oh, maybe you didn't get in the last lick, not personally, maybe someone else did that for you, but you're responsible, along with all the rest of the rumormongers and the snobs and the back-stabbers and the—"

"Just a minute!" Burns yelled. "You don't know what you're saying! Think of what your father did to the school!"

"He did what he thought was best!" Wayne said, his voice

161

breaking. "And look what it got him! No one liked him, no one trusted him, no one took him seriously, no one ever—"

"Did you ever see the man in action?" Burns said. "The way he treated people, the way he humiliated them? The way—"

"It didn't matter!" Wayne said. "He was a wonderful man. He did what he had to to get his chance, and then no one appreciated him. Not even Rogers, the biggest, slimiest hypocrite of all. It didn't matter how my father treated people, or used people. He was still my father!"

Wayne backed away from the couch, and Burns took the opportunity to stand. "Don't you think you might be blinded by that very fact?" he asked.

Wayne was back in control. His voice was light again. "No," he said. "No, I don't. And I'm sorry I let you come here, Dr. Burns. I thought you might really have something to say, but I see that I was wrong. Please. Just go now."

Not knowing what else to say, Burns went.

17

OUTSIDE, BURNS LOOKED at the bare branches of the pecan trees scratching at the sky. He remembered a teacher he had taken a course from when he was an undergraduate, nearly twenty-five years before. The teacher, a widely feared member of the English Department, seemed to believe that the best way to impress a class and to motivate its members to learn was to use intimidation and terror tactics. He had entered the classroom the first day and doused the lights, teaching from then on in semidarkness and telling the students that the light bothered his eyes. He then proceeded to ask a few unanswerable questions of a girl sitting on the front row, harassing her unmercifully, and when he had broken her, moving on to someone else.

The interesting thing was that the man's tactics worked very well for many members of the class. Burns himself had studied like mad every night in case he was to be the next day's victim. He memorized huge chunks of long poems so that he could quote them verbatim on tests. He took scrupulous notes and studied them over and over. He checked books out of the library and read them through, even though they were not required.

Maybe Elmore had been like that, honestly trying to motivate the faculty members to excel and to build up the school through fear and trembling. If so, he had failed. Those methods didn't work any longer, not even with Burns, who would never have dreamed of such an approach in his own classes. Maybe that period of time known as "the sixties" hadn't changed much, but they had changed that.

Of course, they hadn't changed it for everyone. There was always someone around who would perform rather than suffer abuse and who, when abused, would work even harder rather than rebel. Maybe Wayne Elmore was like that, trying to please a father who couldn't be pleased but never ceasing to try. Maybe he really had admired the man and thought everyone else was in the wrong. It certainly wasn't impossible.

Burns got in the green Plymouth and drove away, oddly disturbed but not quite able to say why.

That night Burns had a dream. He had recurring dreams that were probably like those of most teachers. He often dreamed of a particular class that he had once taught, except that in the dream the class was much worse than in reality: students climbed on desks, spoke openly and rudely aloud, threw wads of paper, spit on the floor. As the dream progressed, Burns would find himself growing more and more impatient, more and more frustrated. It always ended with Burns striking a student or hurling a book at one of them. It was not a pleasant dream.

Another dream was of his own student days. He would dream that he was late for an important final exam, and his car wouldn't start. He would begin to run, but he never seemed to arrive anywhere. If the dream went on long enough, he would eventually be walking, then finally crawling, but he would never, ever, arrive for the exam. He would wake up in the mornings after that dream feeling as tired as if he had run a marathon in his sleep.

This dream was different, and in the morning, hanging over his basin and brushing his teeth with mint-flavored Crest, Burns could recall only bits and pieces of it. Wayne Elmore was in it, and his father, but they weren't together. There were doors in the dream, too, lots of doors that kept opening; but Burns could never see what was on the other side of them. Or at least he couldn't remember having seen.

164

Burns spit the Crest foam into the basin and washed his mouth out with cold water. Then he washed his face and shaved. The menthol shaving cream was cold, and the razor scraped his Adam's apple, as it always did. As an English teacher, he was a firm believer in symbolism. He knew that the dream had a meaning. Maybe it would come to him later.

Thursdays were Burns's easy days, only one class, and that one at eight o'clock in the morning. Once that was out of the way, he had the whole day free to read or think or write, or even to go smoke cigarettes in the history lounge. Today, he decided to think.

He was mulling over his list of suspects when he realized that there was one important fact that he had neglected to check. It was a fact that probably had no meaning for Elmore's death, but it was still a fact. Miss Darling's purse was heavy.

Without hesitation, Burns headed for Miss Darling's office. Clem was next door, grading. "Miss Darling in class?" Burns asked, knowing full well that she was.

"Yes," Clem said, making a mark on one of the papers with a red pen before looking up. "You need her for something?"

"No, no," Burns said. "I was just going to borrow a book from her. I'm sure I can find it myself. I'll just have a look."

Miss Darling's office door was open, and Burns stepped in. Because of an unfortunate incident that had occurred several years before, he knew exactly where Miss Darling kept her purse while she was in class. It would be, he was sure, in the bottom desk drawer.

No one at HGC ever locked his or her office door during class hours; it just wasn't done. Everyone trusted everyone else, a system that had worked fairly well for years and years. There had been only one minor deviation in Burns's years at the school—the time when money began to disappear from purses left behind by female teachers. No one mentioned it at first, because no one was really sure that money was disappearing. The thief was not taking all the money, only some of it. A woman might go to the store, reach in her purse to pay for her purchase, and discover that her wallet contained only seventeen dollars instead of the twenty-one dollars she had thought was in there. However hard she might think, she would never be able to remember where the other four dollars had been spent.

There was a good reason why she couldn't remember. The twenty-one dollars had become seventeen not because of unrecalled spending but because of theft. One of the student secretaries, Fox's secretary, in fact, had been the culprit. She would casually walk down the hallways during classes, and if a woman was teaching class and had left her purse behind in plain view, the secretary would slip into the office and dip into the purse for a few dollars.

It was a racket that could have gone on forever without detection, or so it must have seemed to the secretary. But she got unlucky. Two women began talking one day in the rest room, and one mentioned the fact that she couldn't seem to keep up with her money. The other, to their mutual surprise, said that she had the same problem. They mentioned the problem to others and discovered that it was epidemic. They became watchful and hid their purses.

Miss Darling began hanging her purse on a hook attached to the back of her office door, which seemed like a good enough place. One day, her students were working on an in-class theme, and Miss Darling returned to her office to do some grading and catch up on her class preparations. She didn't notice that her open door was not pushed quite so close to the wall as it generally was.

She graded several papers and read over some class notes. She told Burns later that she must have been in the office for twenty or thirty minutes. Then it was time for her to go back to class. She noticed the door for the first time and pushed on it to send it back to the wall. It didn't move far, and there seemed to be something resilient behind it.

Miss Darling looked behind the door. There stood Fox's secretary, still clutching three dollars that she had taken from Miss Darling's purse.

Miss Darling didn't scream or make a scene. She simply took the three dollars from the girl, who tried to tell some story about having found it in the hall—"I was only trying to return it to the rightful owner," she had said—and sent her to the dean of students.

The girl, of course, lost her job and soon left school. Ever after, Miss Darling had hidden her purse in the desk drawer. "Imagine how that poor child must have felt," she told Burns. "Hiding there, hoping that I would leave or that I wouldn't notice her. It must have been terrible. I'll never let anyone go through that again."

Burns, feeling a little like that secretary must have felt on certain occasions, opened the desk drawer. The purse was there. He hefted it. It surely seemed unnecessarily heavy to him.

"Did you find that book?" Clem called from the next office, nearly causing Burns to drop the purse.

"I . . . ah, yes, it's right here," Burns answered. "No problem." He set the purse on Miss Darling's desk. It was genuine leather, black and well-worn. A few cracks in the leather allowed its natural color to show through.

He opened the clasp. Inside there were numerous tissues, a compact, lipstick, a wallet, various odds and ends, and a man's cotton handkerchief. The handkerchief was wrapped around something and the corners were knotted together.

Burns lifted out the handkerchief and its contents. It was quite heavy. He untied the knots.

He was both ashamed and amused when the knots came undone. He almost laughed aloud. The handkerchief was full of coins, mostly quarters. He wondered how many times he had stood in line at the supermarket and been behind a little old lady like Miss Darling. Especially when he was in a hurry. It was then that the little old lady would want to pay her entire bill with change, and she would take what seemed like days getting it out of the purse, untying the knots in the handkerchief, and counting out the exact amount required.

Burns retied the handkerchief, returned it to the purse, and returned the purse to the drawer. He snatched a book off the shelf and walked out, brandishing the book at Clem's doorway. "Got it," he said.

Back in his own office, Burns berated himself unmercifully. He had known Miss Darling was innocent. How could be have made such an ass of himself? At least no one had seen him.

Going over his list of suspects in his mind, they all seemed at least as unlikely as Miss Darling. Coach Thomas? Even Napier had let him go. Dorinda Edgely? Burns knew where the snout had come from, and Dorinda was in the clear. Fox? Tomlin? Clem? Swan? Ridiculous. Somewhere the pattern that he was seeing was flawed. He was going to have to try again, or forget the whole thing.

He sat in his office all morning and through the lunch hour without coming up with any better ideas. He went down and got a Pepsi, but the sugar and caffeine didn't stimulate his thoughts a great deal. In the early part of the afternoon he worked on a list of Faulkner's novels, ranking them from the best to the worst. He was sure that *A Fable* should be on the bottom, but he was never quite sure what to put first. His personal pick was *The Sound and the Fury*, but he felt that he might be making merely the conventional choice and was tempted to replace it with *Absalom, Absalom*. Then there was the problem of *Sanctuary*. Did it belong near the top or near the bottom? Today, he was convinced that it was the top, but he might change his mind tomorrow.

The list kept him occupied for a couple of hours after lunch, but it certainly got him no closer to the answer to the question of who had killed Elmore and why. He also worried about the fires. Who had set them? Why? Were they connected to Elmore's murder? How?

When he left his office at three o'clock, Burns was convinced that he was thinking like a detective. Unfortunately, he wasn't coming up with anything conclusive as a result. He wasn't coming up with anything at all. He planned to go home and see if there were any good movies on the cable that night. He was through worrying about murder and arson.

On the landing near the top of the stairs, there was a large wet stain on the carpet. Attached to the nearby wall was a sign:

PLEASE!
Do Not!!
Bring Canned Drinks!!
into Halls!!!
Maid Rose

Burns had been so wrapped up in his list that he hadn't even heard Rose trying to clean up the mess. It was a never-ending battle between her and the students who wanted to carry their drinks anywhere they went. Whenever anyone spilled so much as a drop, Rose went on the warpath.

Burns chuckled at the sign and started down the stairs. When he reached the second floor, the idea hit him. He stopped in the deserted hall and thought about it. It was something that should have occurred to him before. In questioning those with keys to the Administration Building, Napier would not talk to Rose, but he would question her cousin Nadine. And Rose had a key to the storeroom where someone had gained entrance to Main's attic and attempted to set a blaze.

Burns went back up to his office, unlocked the door, and went in. Sitting at his desk, he tried to think why Rose would want to burn the buildings, or why Nadine would. Of course, it had been neither Rose nor Nadine whom he had encountered in the attic that night, but they might have gotten a friend or a husband to do the actual dirty work.

He tried to call both Mal Tomlin and Earl Fox, but they had left for the afternoon. Trying to get students at HGC to take afternoon classes was an almost impossible task, and hardly anyone stayed past two o'clock since no one ever came by the offices after that time.

Burns kicked back in his chair and put his feet up on the desk, his favorite pose, while he sent his mind roaming through the past. It took a while, but he finally remembered.

It had been quite some time, probably five or six years, and the event had seemed trivial at the time. Rose had turned Elmore in to the traffic court. He had been parking his car behind the Administration Building when he would come by to offer his suggestions for running the school to President Rogers and the current dean. There was really nothing wrong in parking there, but the spots were traditionally reserved for the maintenance crew. More than once, Rose had come back from her break and found Elmore in the only remaining parking spot. Finally, she had complained to the parking crew, and Elmore had been ticketed.

Elmore was furious. He felt that he had a right to park wherever he pleased while on what he termed "official business." He had lost his appeal to the traffic court, appropriately enough, considering his own later actions on that same committee. And he had never forgiven Rose. He had even started a vicious whispering campaign against her during the series of petty thefts that Burns had recalled earlier. He might have succeeded in getting her fired had Miss Darling not caught the thief.

Nadine's troubles with Elmore had been more recent. Nothing was more important to Elmore than his dignity, and he had lost it one day when Nadine had just waxed the hall leading to his office. He had slipped and fallen, sprawling in

170

front of at least two witnesses, both of whom wasted no time in spreading the word. "He looked like a spider trying to fly," was the way one of them had put it to Burns. "Arms and legs just going every which way."

Nadine had suffered Elmore's wrath, but he couldn't get rid of her. After all, she had merely been doing her job. As far as Burns knew, that hall had never been waxed again.

But murder? That was something else. Certainly Rose was stronger than Miss Darling, and perfectly capable of killing Elmore with a swift blow. Nadine, built along the same lines as Rose, could have been the killer just as easily. It seemed to Burns, though, that neither woman had enough of a motive to want to kill Elmore, much less to burn the two buildings. Still, if the buildings were burned, they would never have to be cleaned again. . . .

Burns caught himself. He was starting to weave crazy patterns from very few threads. There was *something* itching at the back of his mind, though, something that just wouldn't quite become clear, and it had to do with Rose. Or her notes. Or . . .

He had it then. He was sure of it. It was obvious, and he was chagrined that he hadn't seen it earlier. He might have been able to save the Administration Building had he only applied himself. Well, it was too late for that, but he could see to it that no more of the college's buildings went up in smoke. He left his office again, this time sure of his direction.

18

AT ELMORE'S HOUSE, Burns stopped the car and looked again at the bare limbs of the pecan trees. Today they reminded him of Hardy's poem about the thrush, something about tangled bine stems that scored the sky. Certainly in the late afternoon the sky was gray enough to fit the occasion.

Burns got out of the car and went up to the porch. He paused with his foot on the step and looked at the swing. Someone must have intended to have a good time there once. He crossed the porch and knocked on the door frame.

Wayne came to the door. "I don't want to talk to you," he said through the screen.

"I'm sorry we got off on the wrong foot last time," Burns said. "I have to talk to you again. This time, I think you'll want to hear what I have to say." Burns felt much more confident than he had felt previously. He was sure he was on the right track now.

"Well, all right," Wayne said, pulling open the interior door.

Burns opened the screen and went inside, seeing the same chairs, the same couch, the same lamp, the same rugs. Nothing at all had changed, but nothing seemed to be the same.

Wayne glided over to the chair. Burns took the couch.

"So," Wayne said. "What is it you want to tell me this time? More about how sorry you are?"

"It's not that at all," Burns said. He took a breath. "I know about the fires."

"Fires?" Wayne asked. He tried to sound puzzled, but Burns could see the flicker in his eyes, just like the flicker in

173

the eyes of a student guiltily denying having cheated on an exam.

"It had to be you, Wayne," Burns said. "Rose was never guilty of leaving a door unlocked, but I'm willing to bet that you had a set of keys to that storeroom on the third floor of Main. Your father had planned for you and a friend to clean it out when it was declared a fire hazard. You never did, but I expect you had the keys."

"That's not true," Wayne said, without force.

"That was you in the attic," Burns said. "You were scared of the rat, and you were angry, so your voice was different, but it was you."

"No," Wayne said.

"I'd also bet you had a set of keys to the Administration Building," Burns said, as if Wayne had not spoken. "Oh, they weren't yours, but I'm sure your father kept a spare set around the house. And you used them."

Wayne stood up, almost as if he'd decided to drop his meek pose and try defiance to see if that worked better. "You 'bet.' You 'expect.' But what can you prove? Not one thing. Nothing. Zero. Zip. Forget it. You may as well leave now."

"Not yet," Burns said, remaining seated. "I can't prove anything, but I think the police can. I think that Maintenance keeps records of people to whom they issue keys, and I'm sure the police will find by checking those records that your father had an extra set of keys to the Administration Building and that he got a key to the storeroom in Main. That may not sound like much to you, but just think what it will sound like to the police."

To tell the truth, it didn't sound like much to Burns, either, not now that he was blurting it out to Wayne in person. It had sounded pretty good in his office, however. "Besides," he said, "you know how hard it is to wash gasoline out of clothes. If the police run a lab check on your clothes, I'm sure they'll find traces of gasoline." He was sure of no such thing, but it sounded good.

174

"That wouldn't be enough," Wayne said.

"With what I'll tell them about the keys, it will," Burns said, relaxing.

Wayne backed away.

"I even think I know why you did it," Burns said.

"No!" Wayne shouted. "You don't know anything!"

"I think I do," Burns said. "You saw how the school felt about your father. Most of the faculty and even most of the students disliked him. When he was killed, there was no big outpouring of sympathy. Why, the only person who liked him must have been Rogers."

"No!" Wayne said again. "Rogers hated him. You don't understand at all!"

"Rogers hated him? But they always seemed—"

"Wait here a minute," Wayne said. "I have something to show you."

This is it, Burns thought. This is where I find out everything. Napier will never believe this. Just wait until I bring in the prisoner.

Wayne came back into the room. His hand was behind his back. He stood looking at Burns.

"Well," Burns said, "show me."

Wayne showed him a small caliber revolver.

Burns felt a chill go down his spine. "Uh, Wayne, this is a joke, right?"

"No, Dr. Burns. It's no joke. This is a .22 revolver, and it's really loaded." He motioned with it slightly.

Burns could see the coppery sheen of the tips of the bullets in the cylinders. "Wayne, you . . ."

"No, Dr. Burns, don't try to say anything. Let me tell you a few things first." Wayne sat in his chair, keeping the gun pointed steadily at Burns. He crossed his legs.

"You should know something about me," Wayne said. "I loved my father. He was a tyrant, and he could be cruel, but he was my father. Lots of people may not understand that, but it's true."

"I understand," Burns said. "I . . ."

Wayne made a small circle with the gun barrel. "Just let me do the talking," he said. "I was a disappointment to my father, in a lot of ways. I never played football. I never ran track. None of those things. My mother always tried to protect me from rough and tumble things like that. Did you ever know my mother, Dr. Burns?"

Burns shook his head. "No. She died just before I came to HGC. I'm sure that she—"

"A simple yes or no will do," Wayne said, like a prosecuting attorney. "If you'd known her, you'd know what I mean. Anyway, I didn't grow up like Mr. Touchdown. I grew up like I am. Not that I mind, really, but it does cause problems sometimes." He stared hard at Burns. "Do you find me effeminate?"

"Ahhh, well . . ."

"That's fine, thanks." Wayne dipped his head in acknowledgment. "I suppose I am. It never really bothered me. Of course, there were jokes, pranks sometimes, but nothing really bad. Not until a few years ago. You wouldn't understand."

"That's where you're wrong," Burns said. Wayne said nothing, so Burns went on. "I understand very well. Don't you realize that I've been an unmarried professor here for years and years? No one trusts an unmarried man, particularly not at a denominational school. There've been all sorts of suspicions about me. I heard the rumors, but I never let them bother me. I like women as much as the next man, but what opportunities did I ever have here? Miss Darling? Besides, I like living alone. It suits me. But it was years before anyone here accepted that."

"Maybe you do understand, a little," Wayne said. "People seem to take for granted that if you don't go out with a girl every week, you're gay. Especially if you have the right mannerisms. It can be a real . . . problem. Girls aren't particularly eager to go out with someone the whole school laughs about."

176

Burns moved forward on the couch. "Well, now that we've got that cleared up . . ."

Wayne waved the pistol at him. "Don't move," he said.

Burns settled back.

"You still don't know everything," Wayne said. "I'm going to tell you how my father got his job. You ever hear anything about that?"

"Just the usual rumors about Rogers," Burns said. "Nothing solid."

"I'll bet," Wayne said with a snort. "I know the rumors, too. The incurable disease bit. Senility. And especially the one about the girl who got knocked up and had to leave town. What a laugh."

Burns wasn't laughing, but then neither was Wayne. "Do you know who started all those rumors?" Wayne asked. "Do you?"

"No," Burns said. "I don't."

"I do," Wayne said. "My father did."

Burns was genuinely surprised. "Your father?"

"That's right. You thought you had it all figured out, didn't you? But you're really not so smart."

"I guess not," Burns said. "I don't understand why your father would start such negative rumors about the president. I don't see at all how that could have possibly helped him get the dean's job." In his curiosity at Wayne's comments, he had almost forgotten about the gun.

Wayne's look was venomous. "It did help him, though. It was all a part of the big lie."

"What big lie?"

"The big lie that got my father his job. The big lie that masked the real truth about Rogers—the one thing that would cost Rogers not only his job but everything else."

Burns edged forward on the couch a bit.

"Don't do that," Wayne said, gesturing with the pistol, reminding Burns of its ugly presence.

"So you know the real truth," Burns said, thinking that he

177

would try to keep Wayne talking. He wasn't sure why, but it always seemed to work in the books. The villains never seemed to realize that all they had to do was pull the trigger and their opposition would topple over. Keep them talking, and something always turned up.

"Yes," Wayne said. "I know the truth."

"So let me in on it," Burns said.

Wayne was silent for a second or two.

"Rogers is a homosexual," he said, finally.

"*What*?" If Burns had been surprised before, he was stunned now.

"You know," Wayne said. "Queer. Gay. Fruit of the loom."

Burns sank back against the couch. "That's . . . well, it's just ridiculous."

"Why? Because he has a wife? What difference does that make?"

"Well, none, I guess, but . . . how do you know he's gay?"

"He made a pass at me," Wayne said.

"A . . . 'pass'?"

"That's what I said. I didn't stutter." Wayne was beginning to get visibly upset.

"It's just that, uh, I don't understand."

"Look, I was in the Administration Building one day. My father had gone over for some reason, and I was looking for him. It was late, and he'd left a few minutes before I got there, but I didn't know that. I went up to Rogers's office. His secretary had already gone home, but he asked me to come in. He talked about my plans, where I was planning to go to school, that kind of stuff. Then he put his hand on me. All right?"

"He . . . he put his hand on you?"

"On my dick!" Wayne yelled. "I was wearing a pair of tight jeans, and he touched me on the dick!"

"Maybe . . . maybe it was an accident," Burns said weakly.

"Accident! *Accident*? What a load of shit!" Wayne got out

178

of the chair and paced in front of the couch.

"You told your father?"

"Of *course* I told him! Of course!"

"He used you," Burns said. "He used you to get the job. And he told Rogers that his secret would always be safe."

Wayne turned and brandished the pistol over the top of the coffee table. "How could my father do that?" he yelled.

"I . . ." Burns said.

"Never mind," Wayne said, suddenly strangely calm. It was an amazing transformation. "It doesn't matter now. Nothing matters now. Get up."

"What?"

"Get . . . up!" Wayne waved the pistol upward.

Burns got up.

"Walk through there." Wayne pointed to the doorway with the gun barrel.

Not knowing exactly what to expect, Burns walked through the door. There was a short hall with doorways on the right, left, and at the end. The doors on the right and at the end were closed.

"Go in the kitchen," Wayne said, jabbing him in the ribs.

Burns turned left. The kitchen was small, with white-painted wooden cabinets. The appliances were also white. At one end was a breakfast area furnished with a plain wooden table and chairs that looked as if they might have come from a place named Furniture Mart.

"Sit at the table," Wayne said. His voice was still calm, almost cold. Burns tried to remember if it was the third or fourth voice Wayne had used. He sat in one of the wooden chairs.

Wayne hit him very hard in the side of the head with the pistol.

Burns didn't quite fall out of the chair, slumping instead against the table. It was as if he were there but not there. He didn't black out, but he wasn't aware of anything in particular, either.

179

He felt himself being jerked upright, and his arms were being pulled behind the chair. He was vaguely aware of pain, mostly in his head. He tried to clear it by shaking it, which only made the pain much worse.

The next thing he remembered was Wayne holding ice cubes wrapped in a towel at the base of his neck.

"Feeling better, Dr. Burns?" Wayne asked, as solicitous as if he were the faithful family physician.

"Ughrrm," Burns mumbled.

"Fine, fine," Wayne said. "There's going to be another fire, I'm afraid, Dr. Burns. And this time you're going to be in it. You missed the other two by such a little bit, I know you're disappointed. This time you'll be right in the thick of things."

Wayne walked over to the kitchen stove. "It's really sad," he said, "that so many accidents happen in the home, quite a few in the kitchen, actually."

"Arson in . . . ves . . . ti . . . gation," Burns said.

"Yes, well, I suspect that there's hardly enough of the Administration Building left to give them much of a clue, though they know I was in Main, thanks to you. And I'll just say that all the fires are the product of some vicious mind attempting to get revenge on my father for some imagined slight. Almost anyone would believe that, don't you think."

Burns didn't try to answer.

"Dr. Burns," Wayne said. "Burns. What an appropriate name. I can see the headlines now: 'BURNS BURNS.' It has a certain ring to it."

"Wayne . . ." Burns said.

"I'm really sorry," Wayne said, lapsing back into his breathy voice. "I really am. If there were any other way to handle this, I'd do it, but there just isn't. I can't let you go around telling things about me, can I?"

"I . . . guess . . . not," Burns said. He was too weak and drained to argue, especially with someone as crazy as Wayne. He wondered if Wayne had ever really loved his father at all,

180

or if that was just another disguise that he had adopted.

Wayne left the room and returned with a can of gasoline. "I've learned a lot about starting fires, most of it by experience," he said. "Main didn't burn right because I didn't use enough gasoline and because that old attic was far too drafty. The Administration Building was much easier; it was almost airtight and the fumes weren't dissipated. It's the fumes that ignite, you know."

Burns didn't know, but he didn't say so. Wayne sloshed the gas out of the can.

"It may be that when they find what's left of your body, assuming that there's enough to identify," Wayne said, "they'll think it was you who set the fire. Of course, I'll be as surprised as anyone that you could have held such a grudge against my father, but, after all, you were the one who reported the attempted burning of Main and the successful one of the Administration Building. Everyone knows how arsonists like to watch the blazes they create. You just got too close to this one."

As he talked, Wayne was spreading gasoline around the kitchen. He emptied the red and yellow can and returned with another one.

"This old house isn't very airish," he said. "This smell is giving me a headache."

It was giving Burns a headache, too, not to mention scaring him pretty badly. He was too weak to make much of an attempt even to move, but he tried. His hands were bound behind the chair.

Wayne finished pouring the gasoline out of the second can. He walked over and closed the door to the other room. "What's going to happen is pretty simple. I'm going to walk out that door"—he pointed to the back door, the one that led from the kitchen to the outside—"and when I get out there, I'm going to toss a match in here. I suspect that you can figure out the rest."

Burns struggled weakly, but it was no use, even though he

had no trouble figuring out the rest.

Wayne went out and closed the door. Burns wondered for a moment how he was going to throw in the match. Then Wayne tapped out one of the four small window panes at the top of the door.

"Ta-ta," Wayne said. He walked a few steps away and flicked a cigarette lighter. He tossed it toward the hole.

Burns heard a crash behind him, and then the world exploded.

19

SOMETIME LATER, BURNS was never sure just how long, he woke up on a stretcher.

He opened his eyes. Boss Napier towered above him.

"See, I told you he was fine," Napier said to a white-suited paramedic. "A little oxygen and the guy's as good as new."

Burns's throat was raw, but he tried to talk. "Wha' . . .?"

"Like I say, you're in great shape," Napier said. "Maybe a few cuts from the flying glass when I chunked the garbage can through the kitchen window, but aside from that you don't have a thing to worry about. You'll probably be back in school tomorrow."

"H-h-h . . .?"

"How? Hell, everybody knows an explosion follows the line of least resistance. So when that stuff blew up, it just tossed you back through that window I broke. You're a little singed up, but nothing like you would've been if you'd stayed in there. Course, we called the fire department, and the fire's almost out now. Lucky for you I came along."

"Ah-h-h . . .?"

"The kid?" Napier gave a satisfied smile. "Don't worry about him. We got him. You know, Bonz, it's a good thing I worried about you turning up at the scenes of all the fires and the murder like I did. Otherwise, I'd never have put the tail on you. Not that I ever really suspected that *you* were involved in anything fishy. Not at all. It's just that you kept turning up everywhere."

Napier paused and looked at Burns earnestly, as if to make sure that he was being heard. "Anyway, like I said, I put a tail on you. He was watching this house tonight, and when you stayed in there so long he gave me a call. I came right on out, of course, and sort of looked the place over. When I saw you tied up in that chair, I had reason to think that I could legally enter the house. Looked like the quickest way in was through that window, so I heaved the garbage can."

Burns wanted to say that he thought Napier had cut it kind of close, but what came out was something like, "Ooo cussus cloos."

"Right," Napier said. "I don't blame you for feeling grateful, but don't thank me. I guess I sort of owe you an apology, and after all you've led us right to the killer and the arsonist."

"Aroo sheerr?"

"Right," Napier said. "You just take it easy. You'll be just fine in the morning."

The paramedics carted Burns away. He didn't remember much about the ambulance ride to the hospital.

As it turned out, Burns *was* pretty much all right by the next morning. There were a few minor cuts from the glass, a lot of bruises, and his wrists were rubbed pretty raw, but his voice was almost back to normal. It had been a terrifying experience, but it hadn't damaged him permanently.

Climbing the stairs in Main, Burns tried to think of the ways it could have been worse. He could have been burned to death in a fire. He could have been asphyxiated. Main could have burned. Elmore could still be alive.

No, strike that last thought. It was uncharitable. Put it down to the soreness he still felt in his arms from their being tied behind his back. He was alive, his building was still standing, and he was glad of both things. On his way in, he had seen the rubble that had once been the Administration Building. What if he had lost his books, notes, desk, typewriter? It would have been devastating. Somehow it seemed right that Elmore's building had burned instead.

After his first class, he sneaked past Clem and Miss

184

Darling and went down to the history lounge. Mal Tomlin and Fox were there, smoking and waiting to hear the scoop. The arrest of Wayne Elmore had made the morning news programs on the Pecan City radio stations, and so had Burns's part in it.

"I always thought he looked like a sneaky little shit," Tomlin said, "but I didn't know he was a nut case."

Burns took a Bel-Air from Fox. "A nut case?"

"Have to be," Fox said, giving Burns a light. "Why else would he do that stuff?"

"I'm not really sure," Burns said, taking a deep drag. "I have a feeling Napier will be by to talk to me about it all today, and maybe he's found out something more. I have to admit that I think you're right about the 'nut case' bit. The boy is definitely strange."

That led to a discussion of a possible insanity defense, which led to several more cigarettes. Then Burns had to go to his ten o'clock class. "Keep in touch," Fox said as Burns left the room. "We want to be in on all the latest rumors."

"Not much danger of that not happening," Burns said, heading for the stairs.

At eleven o'clock, Napier was waiting in Burns's office, still puffing a bit from the climb. He was already sitting down.

Burns put his books on the desk and sat behind it. "Well, Chief, what can I do for you?"

"Not much," Napier said. "I think we've just about got things wrapped up." He smiled, a disconcerting grimace that Burns did his best to ignore. "There is just one little problem, though."

Burns had been afraid of that. "What is it?" he asked.

"The kid won't admit a thing," Napier said. "Not the murder, not the arson, nothing."

"I see what you mean," Burns said.

"So we thought maybe you could help us out," Napier said.

"Oh? How?" Burns was beginning to enjoy himself.

Napier was not smiling now. He knew that Burns was playing a game, but he didn't want to let on. "By telling me what happened at Elmore's," he said.

"You mean, did he admit anything to me?"

"That's what I mean."

Burns decided to stop kidding around. "Yes," he said.

Napier leaned forward with a predatory look. "What?"

"Let me tell you something first," Burns said. He told him about the keys and their availability.

"Damn," Napier said. "I should have thought of that."

"Well," Burns said, "you didn't know about Elmore hiring his son to clean the storeroom."

"Yeah, there's that," Napier said. "Now, what else. I mean, what did he tell you?"

"Not much," Burns said. "He did admit that he was the one in Main when I caught him in the attic. Actually, that's about all."

Napier did not look pleased. "Nothing about why he did it? Nothing about his father?"

"No," Burns said, "and that's been bothering me. The first time I talked to him, he seemed genuinely to admire his father." Burns was holding back important information, he knew, but he couldn't see how it would help Napier to know everything Wayne had said. Burns himself hadn't decided exactly how he felt about it.

"He's a fruitcake," Napier said. "That tells you a lot about how much you can believe him."

"You're apparently willing to believe that he was telling the truth about being in Main," Burns said. "Why not believe he admired his father?"

"Because it doesn't fit," Napier said. "Not that it matters. We can get him for attempted murder for trying to knock you off, and we can get him for the fires. With all that against him, we may not even need to get him for killing his father."

"Still . . ."

"Yeah, I'd still like to know. I'd like to have a weapon and a motive. But I'll take what I can get. You'll testify, of course."

Burns was not thrilled at the prospect, but he felt that he really had no choice. "Yes," he said.

Napier stood up. "If you can think of anything else that might help, let us know. We're going to give the DA a solid case even if the kid does try to get out of it with an insanity plea."

"I'll be in touch," Burns said. He did not get up. Napier nodded and left the office.

Burns stayed in his office to grade papers rather than going to lunch. He was slightly behind, and he always liked to return papers promptly. He did not make much progress because he kept answering the telephone. Coach Thomas called, and Dorinda Edgely called, both to thank him for his part in finding the killer. They sounded relieved and happy. Don Elliott called to say that he hoped his part in selecting Elmore could be kept quiet. Burns assured him that his sinecure as dormitory supervisor was safe. He would have liked to do something about Elliott, but there was really nothing he could do. And who was to say that he wouldn't have done the same thing had he been presented with the same temptations?

Clem and Miss Darling poked their heads in to say that they had learned of his exploits by listening to local newscasts, but neither stayed very long. Miss Darling did mention that she hoped that all of Elmore's evil schemes for ruining HGC had died with him. Burns told her that he was pretty sure they had.

He got bored with grading after a couple of hours and started fooling around with his lists. He opened his middle drawer and located the one he had started so long before, the one headed *Things I Hate*, and looked it over. There, with its arrow pointing to somewhere near the top of the list, was Elmore's name. Even now, his influence was hard to escape. Burns took his Pilot Precise Ball Liner out of the drawer and made a wavy line through the name. There was no need to hold a grudge any longer. It was time to start putting things behind him.

Unfortunately, the longer Burns stared at the list, the more he became fascinated with the name that he had crossed out. Elmore had been such a malign influence in the lives of so many people that it was a shame to see him go, at least in some ways. What were people going to talk about, now that he was gone?

Although Wayne seemed quite willing to continue to talk about his father. Burns still couldn't shake the feeling that Wayne had been sincere when he had defended the dead dean. Of course, he had his own speculation, which he had concealed from Napier. Elmore had indeed despitefully used his own son, making Wayne's encounter with Rogers the basis for his promotion. And then he had kept his son on campus rather than sending him to another school, displaying him, so to speak, as a constant reminder to Rogers that Elmore was the one with the real power.

But was Wayne telling the truth? He seemed to be going through so many personalities at about that time that Burns wasn't sure what to believe or disbelieve.

And if he chose to believe Wayne, what was his obligation to the school? Burns didn't particularly care whose *schlong* Rogers grabbed, as long as it didn't belong to Burns, but homosexuality was one of the unforgivable sins at HGC. If Rogers made a wrong move, he could cost thousands and maybe millions of dollars in financial support from churches and ministers. But Burns didn't know whom to tell, even if he wanted to tell. The board? Even a hint of such a thing could ruin Rogers forever, and if Wayne had been lying, Burns would be guilty of spreading a ruinous falsehood.

At about that point in Burns's ruminations, Bunni came in. "Gee, Dr. Burns," she said, "you're famous. It's really neat having someone like you for a teacher. All the kids are

188

talking about it." She paused for breath. "We kind of feel sorry for Wayne, though."

"Did you happen to see Wayne that day you were picketing, Bunni?"

"You mean, did he picket with us?" Bunni was clearly puzzled that Burns would ask such a question.

"No, no," Burns said. "I mean, did you see him go in the building?"

"I didn't see anybody go in," Bunni said. "Except for Miss Darling, like I told you."

"It was just a thought," Burns said. "I guess none of the picketers went in, not George or anyone like that?"

"No," Bunni said. "We were all too interested in making sure we did a good job of marching in front of the building and getting the signs where they could be seen from the street. Nobody had time to go inside."

"I'm glad the picketing was orderly," Burns said. "There could have been trouble otherwise."

Bunni looked at him.

"What I mean is that if things had gotten rowdy, some of you might have gotten in trouble with the police. They might even have accused some of you of killing Dean Elmore."

"Oh," Bunni said. "Well, some of us got in trouble anyway."

"What?" Burns asked. "How?"

"We were late for assembly," Bunni said. "We waited until everyone had left the building and until there was no one around but us, so we could be sure everyone had seen the signs, and then we went on over. But the roll checkers had already taken attendance by the time we got there. George is trying to raise his grade-point average a little bit by having a perfect attendance record in assembly, so we had to find the checker for our section and tell her that we weren't absent, just a little late. It was all a big hassle."

"I see what you mean," Burns said.

"That's not all," Bunni said. "The really unfair thing is that

189

assembly got started late. We got there before the opening prayer, so it wasn't fair for them to count us late. The checkers ought to wait for the prayer instead of just going by the time."

"Late is late," Burns said, hating himself for mouthing the party line.

"I guess. Anyway, I hope all the excitement is over for a while. George and I really need to concentrate on our studies."

"You help George a lot, do you?" Burns asked.

"Not too much," Bunni said. "Now that football season's over, he'll do all right. He just needs the time." She got up to leave. "See you tomorrow."

"Yes," Burns said. "See you then." As Bunni left, he looked down at his desk top at the list of *Things I Hate*. Bunni had walked in when he had been writing Elmore's name the other time. He wondered how high up Elmore's name would be on other, similar lists. What if Miss Darling had one, or Earl Fox, or Abner Swan, or President Rogers?

He thought about that for a while, and then he got up and went downstairs.

20

BURNS STOOD LOOKING at the spot formerly occupied by the Administration Building. The walls had been pushed down, and a front-end loader was noisily dumping a cascade of burned bricks into the rear of a dump truck. The bricks were being hauled away to a nearby field, and there were plans to level the ground and plant grass where Hartley Gorman II had stood. If the board could raise the money, a new Administration Building would be erected on the same site, but that would be several years in the future.

As the dump truck rattled away, Burns walked on by. There were only a few students visible on the campus in the afternoon, and most of them were idly watching the front-end loader and the dump trucks, another of which backed up for its bricks.

The administration's new offices were in the former warehouse of a wholesale hardware firm that had gone out of business a year or two before. The owners had offered the space after the fire, and Rogers had gladly accepted. The warehouse was practically on the campus, right at the western edge, so it was an easy walk.

Burns entered the cavernous building and walked through it to the offices located at the rear. His footsteps on the cement floor echoed off the brick walls and the high tin roof.

The doors at the back were all alike, dull brown wood with tarnished handles. Each one had an index card taped to it giving the occupant's name and position. Burns knocked on the one that read "A. Clark Rogers, President."

"Come in," Rogers's secretary called.

Burns opened the door and went in, startled as usual by the secretary's upswept glasses, which seemed doubly incongruous because of her gray hair. "I'd like to see Dr. Rogers," he said.

"Just a moment," the secretary said. "I'll see if he's free." She stepped around a partition that extended across most of the back of the room. It wasn't a private office, exactly, but it would do in a pinch.

This office wasn't furnished very well, no overstuffed chairs, no pictures on the walls, no carpet on the floor. Just a worn desk and chair, probably scavenged from some old office furniture that had been in storage for years.

The secretary returned. "Dr. Rogers will see you now," she said.

Burns went around the partition. Rogers was seated at another worn desk. There was a straight-backed wooden chair for visitors. Rogers shook hands with Burns and asked him to be seated. "Terrible thing about young Elmore," he said. "Your role in the whole affair speaks well for you, however, and I want you to know that you're high on my list of candidates to replace the late Dean Elmore. Very high on my list."

"No, thanks," Burns said. "I don't think so."

"What, tied to the classroom?" Rogers asked. "I felt that way myself, years ago, when I first moved into administration. But you might be surprised if you gave it a try."

"That's not it, not really," Burns said. "It's just that I don't think you're going to be appointing anyone."

"What?" Rogers's usually pleasantly ruddy face seemed to pale slightly. "What do you mean?"

"I mean I think I know what happened in Elmore's office when he was killed. I think I know who killed him."

"Well, of course. Of course. The police . . . young Elmore . . . the arrest . . ." Blustering didn't become Rogers, and he ran down quickly.

"I don't mean Wayne Elmore," Burns said. "Oh, he

192

burned the Administration Building, no doubt about that. And he tried to burn Main. But he didn't kill his own father. I'm not sure he knows who did, but I think he burned the building to retaliate against the school. He blames all of us for his father's death, and he wanted to strike back somehow. That's why he tried for Main first. The loss of that old building would really have hurt, and it would have hurt us all. But I happened to stop him. So then he went for the second-oldest building. That time he got it."

"But I thought he confessed," Rogers said.

"No. He hasn't made any statement. When he does, I expect that the police will turn up here. Napier may be slow, but he's not as slow as I am. I should have known immediately."

Rogers was toying with a letter opener. It was shiny and new, probably a promotional item that he'd gotten to furnish his new office. "Known what?"

"That you killed Elmore."

Rogers put the letter opener down. "Don't be ridiculous."

"Oh, it's not ridiculous. You must have hated him for years, what with the way he blackmailed himself into the dean's job."

"How . . .?"

"Don Elliott gave me a strong hint. Wayne told me why."

Rogers leaned back as if deflated. "It wasn't what you think," he said.

"It doesn't matter what I think," Burns said. "It's what Wayne and his father thought. It's that you asked Elliott to assure Elmore's appointment as dean."

"I had to," Rogers said. "He would have ruined me."

"I guess it was the degree mill business that did it," Burns said.

"That and the attack on the sports program," Rogers said. There was no more pretense. "I simply went to his office to talk to him, to ask him to moderate his views, reconsider his ideas. He . . . he talked to me as if I were scum, as if I were

193

nothing. He called me an old fool." Rogers's face sagged. "I suppose he was right."

"So you hit him."

"So I hit him. There was a big glass paper-clip holder right there on the desk. I picked it up and hit him. I didn't mean to kill him. I suppose it was God's will."

Burns couldn't believe his ears. "God's will? Was it God's will that you let Coach Thomas sit in jail for what you'd done? Were you going to let Wayne Elmore take the blame for you?"

Rogers put his hands on the desk and steepled the fingers piously. "I told the Lord that if Coach Thomas was not released I would confess," he said. "I made the same statement with regard to young Elmore."

"I can't believe this," Burns said. "The president of a school like this one, striking bargains with God."

"There is ample precedent," Rogers said.

"Not in my book," Burns said, rising to his feet.

Rogers's hand dropped to the desk and rose with the letter opener. Its sharp tip pointed at Burns's stomach.

"Don't be a fool," Burns said.

Rogers dropped the letter opener and stood up, walking around his desk. "Join me in prayer," he said. "Let's get down right here and pray for guidance." He stooped to his knees.

"You pray," Burns said. "I have a phone call to make."

As he rounded the partition, he could hear Rogers's voice, calling on the Lord and asking for guidance and forgiveness. Rogers's secretary was looking at Burns with a mixture of fear and disgust.

"Don't blame me," Burns said as he went out. "He should have gotten to assembly on time." His footsteps echoed hollowly as he walked through the empty warehouse.

Fox was wearing a garish plaid sport coat and white shoes. He was tipped back comfortably in one of the rickety chairs in the history lounge, smoking a nonfiltered Lucky Strike. "I

194

figured, 'What the hell,' " he said, offering one to Burns. "If you're gonna smoke, you might as well *smoke*. Live dangerously. Devil may care."

Burns took the cigarette. "Don't tell me," he said. "Let me guess. Abner Swan had a garage sale."

"Damn," Fox said. "You really are a pretty good detective. How'd you know that?"

"Never mind," Burns said. "It's too complicated a chain of deduction to explain." He lit the Lucky, took a deep drag, and nearly choked to death on the spot. "Good grief," he coughed. "These things are potent."

"What's potent?" Mal Tomlin asked, coming in the door.

"Luckies," Fox said. "Want one?"

"No, thanks," Tomlin said. "I've got my own."

Burns tried another drag, shallower this time. He made it without choking. Then he noticed the big change in the lounge's decor. "You bought a real ashtray," he said.

"That's right," Fox said proudly. In the center of the dilapidated card table there was a greenish ceramic alligator with a long depression in its back. "I couldn't resist it. Picked it up at a little garage sale for just a quarter. It was a steal."

"I always sort of liked the aluminum cans," Burns said.

"You'll get used to it," Tomlin said.

"I wonder if we could get us a new president at a garage sale?" Fox said.

"Burns would probably just get something on him and put him away," Tomlin said. "More bad publicity for the school."

Rogers's arrest had stirred up considerable media interest, especially combined with Wayne Elmore's story. HGC was getting more air time than the president of the United States, as well as a good bit of ink in the major metropolitan newspapers. The trials promised to be quite sensational.

"You going to open up a detective agency?" Fox asked.

"Hardly," Burns said. "If Bunni hadn't come by the office to talk, I might never have thought of Rogers as a killer. He had plenty of motive, but I really thought Wayne had done

195

it. The way his father treated him, he seemed like the logical choice. Especially after I found out the reason Elmore got to be our dean."

"I bet you could get a lot of business if you did, though," Fox said. "You looked pretty good on TV the other night."

"Yeah," Tomlin said, "but you would have looked even better if Earl had let you borrow his sport jacket."

"You like this, huh? Bet you'd never guess where I got it."

"Well, let's see," Tomlin said. "Ten to one, Abner Swan had a garage sale recently."

Fox looked hurt and surprised. "Burns told you," he said.

"No, he didn't," Tomlin said. "I have detective instincts, too."

Burns stubbed out his Lucky in the alligator's back. "I think I'll go down and see The Rat," he said.

"I think I'll go with you," Tomlin said. "There's something I want to check on."

"Me, too," Fox said.

They all trooped down to the men's room.

When they got inside, Burns understood why they had come. The Rat was slipping down farther and farther. About half of him was visible, now. The combination of the poison and the dry air of Pecan City had dried him out so completely that his body was practically flat.

"I think it's time," Tomlin said.

"Not for me," Fox said. "No way in the world I'm touching that thing."

Burns walked over to the towel dispenser and pulled down the handle three or four times, then ripped off the length of brownish paper towel that extended downward. "Allow me," he said. He put the towel around one of The Rat's paws and pulled. The dead rodent slipped easily from its place behind the board.

"Maybe we ought to give it to Rose," Fox said.

"Don't be a wise guy or I'll throw it on you," Burns said, carrying it to the trash can and laying it carefully inside. Then

196

he covered it with the paper towel. "One less rat," he said.

"Three less," Tomlin said. "Let's go."

"Come on down and have another Lucky when you're done," Fox said. "It's the least I can do for you."

Burns smiled. "I'll be there," he said.

If you have enjoyed this book and would like to receive details of other Walker mystery titles, please write to:
Mystery Editor
Walker and Company
720 Fifth Avenue
New York, NY 10019